Love & Adventure

Holidays in Hallbrook

Elsie Davis

Sweet Romance Publishing

Sweet Romance Publishing

Sweetromancepublishing.com

PO Box 778

Liberty, NC 27298

It's all about the kids...
To Lydia and Liam Butler...the funny, endearing
voices of the children who narrate
the Holidays in Hallbrook series
To Gabriella (Gabby) and William (Trey) Re-
sendes...my two oldest grandchildren...who add
so much love and laughter to my life

A special shout out and thank you to Billye Hern-
don who suggested the name Lynette, and to the
reader (thank you S.G) who suggested the name
Connor in the Name the Character's contest.

Proverbs: 22:6
Start children off on the way they should go,
and even when they are old they will not turn
from it.

Chapter One

♥

"YOU ALMOST READY TO go, Trey?" Connor asked his son as they passed each other in the hall.

"Yup. Just need to double-check my tackle box and rod to make sure I've got what I need." Fishing was something the two of them had in common. Well, that and baseball. But it was the bass and catfish that were on their brains for this weekend's camping trip to White Mountain State Park.

"I've already done that. We're all loaded and ready to go. Make sure you've got extra clothes. With all the torrential rains we've had the past few days, things are sure to be wet, and you never know when they'll come in handy." The trip had been a spontaneous decision knowing tomorrow was a teacher workday, something a PE teacher didn't have to worry about when it came to catching up, grading papers, and planning lessons.

"Okay. I sure hope we get a good site near the lake."

"Me too, but with all the rain, some of those won't be useable." It was only because of the bad weather that Connor felt confident they'd be able to score one of the first-come, first-serve sites available, especially given the decision to leave today after school. Come Friday morning, last-minute outdoor enthusiasts would be rushing to get there, hoping to still get a site for the weekend.

Connor watched as his son headed back down the hall and disappeared into his room. The trip was his way of trying to find a way to connect with his son. Trey had struggled this past year with the divorce after his mother left Hallbrook and New Hampshire altogether, choosing to start her life over in Texas. A life without a husband, her son, or anything else that would tie her down and cramp her newfound freedom.

He rechecked his list, not wanting to forget any-thing they might need—right down to the bear nets to keep their food safe from grizzlies and raccoons.

It wasn't the first time he'd considered switching up the routine and giving in to the urge to buy a camper.

Connor eyed his baseball glove and ball on the coffee table, not wanting to leave it behind but knowing it wouldn't be a part of the back-woods experience. Four days without working on his pitching skills didn't happen often. Baseball was his life, or it had been until he blew out his arm and had to recuperate from surgery.

Now, his life was spent teaching Physical Education to a bunch of middle-school children who preferred to be anywhere but in gym class. Outside of school, his focus was on raising Trey and trying to get his arm and body back in shape for the next time the minor league had tryouts close to home. One day, he promised himself, he'd be back in the minors, and with any luck, finally get his chance at the majors with the Boston Red Sox.

Connor made his way out to the garage to grab a couple of extra flashlights and some fire-starter logs. Wet wood and ground would make fire starting 101 look like an advanced class. He was all for the naturalist method of doing things, but common sense told him a side guarantee wouldn't hurt if they planned on cooking meals over a hot fire.

His phone rang, and he stopped to pull it out of his back pocket. Keith, his neighbor and closest friend, was calling. "Hey there. What's up?" Connor asked.

"Are you still home? I'm in a jam and was hoping there was some way you could help me." Keith didn't usually ask for anything. And considering all the favors he did for Connor by helping with Trey, he'd do about anything for the guy.

"Name it and consider it done," Connor said, knowing it was true.

Keith chuckled. "I like the sound of that, but I'm not sure you should go around agreeing until you hear what it is I'm asking. Or I might hold you to it."

"What's up? I reckon as long as you're not asking me to cancel my camping trip with Trey, we're good." He knew Keith well enough to know any request would be within reason.

"*Hmmm.* Definitely not a cancel request. Far from it. Are you still in town, or have you left already?" his friend asked.

"We're still here. Probably ten minutes or so from heading out. Why?" Connor glanced up as Trey tossed his phone on the front seat of the truck and headed back into the house.

"Well, like I said, I'm in a jam. Feel free to say no, but I don't have many options, so I thought I'd ask. The thing is, my niece is here for a few days."

"I remember you telling me she was coming and that your sister is moving back into town." The woman had lost her husband a year ago in an accident, and this was her attempt to put her life back together. Something Connor understood all too well.

"Yes, well, Lynette is still wrapping things up in Boston. I just got a call, and there's an emergency at one of the plants in Pennsylvania. They need me to fly down there and handle it. I'm not sure how long I'll be gone, and my sister won't be here until Sunday. The problem is, I can't very well take Gabby with me."

"That *is* a tough spot. What is it you want me to do?" Connor asked.

"Take her camping with you," Keith said, his words dropping like a bomb.

"You're kidding, right?" It was no wonder his friend had issued the warning about accepting too fast. He didn't know the first thing about the girl, or even taking care of girls in general. "Does she even like to camp?" he asked, trying to wrap his brain around the request.

"Loves it. She's into outdoorsy things, and she loves baseball. You two wouldn't have a shortage of things to discuss." More than likely, his friend meant softball, but now wasn't the time to correct him.

There was no way Connor could say no, and he knew it. Keith watched Trey all the time when he needed a hand, and a turnabout was in order. Not to mention, helping a friend was the right thing to do. "This was really supposed to be a father-son trip, but of course, we'll take her," he said, mentally trying to shift gears. "I can throw some more food in with the supplies and grab the larger tent since the one I packed is only a two-man pup tent." It would push their departure back a bit, but it shouldn't take long to get what he needed for the girl. He'd make this work—somehow.

"You do realize I'm not going to try and talk you out of it," Keith said, the relief evident in his voice. "Thank you so much. I'll have her throw some things together in a backpack and be right over to introduce you all."

"Fair enough. See you in a few." The first order of business was to tell Trey since he was certain the change in plans wouldn't be to his liking. Heck, Connor wasn't sure *he* liked the change in plans, but he was adult enough to roll with it. His son, not so much.

"Trey?" Connor called out.

"We leaving?" Trey asked, coming into the living room.

"*Ummm*, not yet," Connor said, searching for the right words. "You see, there's been a slight change in plans." Huge understatement.

Trey frowned, his shoulders slumped with defeat. "Now what? Let me guess...we're not going. I should have known you'd back out."

"Not quite. Keith called, and he needs to go out of town on a work emergency. His niece is visiting for a few days, and he wanted me to keep an eye on her until her mother gets here Sunday. So…I've agreed to take her with us."

Trey did a double-take. "Take a girl on our trip? Are you kidding me? This is a guy's trip. No girls allowed. Call him back and tell him she can't come."

"I've already said yes, but at least we can still go camping," Connor said, trying to let the kid down gently.

"Then I'm not going." Trey crossed his arms and glared back at Connor, an insolent expression on his face. It was the same attitude issue he had dealt with for the past year, the one he'd hoped to bridge this weekend. Unfortunately, bonding would need to wait until the Father's Day camping trip next month.

"You don't have the option of staying home alone. So, either way, here or at the campground, his niece is staying with us. So what's it going to be? Camping and fishing with a girl tagging along, or house-bound and watching movies with a girl?" Trey had left him no choice but to back him into a corner.

Trey shrugged. "Fine. I'll go, but I don't have to like it." No surprise, given the circumstances.

"That's true, but I do expect you to be courteous and make her feel welcome." It was better to set the rules in advance than have it out with his son in front of the Gabriella.

"Whatever." Trey rolled his eyes.

The doorbell rang. Connor opened the door to let Keith and his niece inside.

"Thanks again, Connor. This is Gabriella Taylor. Gabby, this is Connor Weston and his son, Trey," Keith said, making the introductions.

"Hi," the girl said, a troubled look on her face. She didn't want to do this either. If that was the case, this was going to be a long weekend.

"It's nice to meet you. I heard you like being outdoors, so hopefully, you'll have fun with us. Ever do any fishing?" Connor asked, trying to give Trey time to recover and at least say hello.

"No." Gabby shrugged. She looked to be about ten years old, but with the weight of the world on her shoulders.

Keith stood there, looking unsure of what to do next.

This was one of those times he needed to step up and take control. "They'll be fine. I'm sure we'll all have fun once we get settled and start catching fish and communing with Mother Nature," Connor said, trying to reassure his friend. Trey still hadn't said a word, much to his chagrin. "All right, you two. Let's get a move on. I've got to grab a couple of things. Trey, if you'll take Gabby's bag and stow it in the back of the truck, I'll lock up the house, and we can head out."

Trey glared at him, and for a moment, Connor thought he was going to argue the point. Instead, he took the bag from Gabby and headed for the door. "Come on, it's this way," he said in a brisk voice. Any form of communication at this point was a start.

"Are you sure this is okay? I'm really sorry if it's upset your weekend with Trey," Keith said.

"I promise you it'll be fine. How hard can it be to have one extra mouth to feed and one extra line to bait?" Connor wasn't expecting it to be all laughter and cozy family time, but he also wasn't expecting it to be a total disaster. Camping was camping, something he enjoyed no matter what the circumstances.

"Okay, then. I'm out of here. I've got a plane to catch. Call me if you need anything. And here's Lynette's number. I've left her a message with the change of plans to keep her in the loop since she didn't answer her phone." Keith handed him a folded-up piece of paper.

"Sounds good." His friend left, and Connor went about grabbing extra food, a pillow, a blanket, another sleeping bag, and the larger tent. With everything loaded, they were ready to go, the kids already in the truck, each one avidly playing games on their phones and ignoring one another.

Wait till they lost cell and internet service.

Lynette locked the front door and turned to walk to her car, her heart heavy with the finality of the sale of the house. It was the end of her and Gabby's life in the military, or that of a military family, and all the chaos that came with it. Dirk's decorated service to his country as an Air Force soldier had all come to a screeching halt with his accidental death.

Every day he'd been deployed, she had worried about something happening, never expecting anything to go wrong right here on U.S. soil, and especially not on the base where he worked.

A mechanical problem. At least that's how the officer who came to deliver the heartbreaking news explained it. The minute the man had shown up in full-dress uniform, she'd known something was wrong.

Lynette had wanted to rage at the world when it happened, but now, a year later, she just wanted it over. The guilt of knowing she wasn't happy in her marriage plagued her daily. Dirk and she had grown apart, his long absences taking a toll on the family. Some enlisted men and their families found ways to remain more settled, but not Dirk. He thrived on change and had no problem uprooting the family each time something new landed in his lap with an opportunity to move up the ranks.

She, on the other hand, had grown to hate it. And it wasn't just her. Gabby hadn't liked changing schools and moving any more than Lynette. Not that it mattered. They both did what was expected of them as the supportive military family they'd been groomed to be—outwardly anyway.

It had taken a while to come to terms with the changes, not that she would ever fully understand. Trusting God with the weight of her world, she had slowly begun to heal and come to terms with her new reality. Lynette would always miss the man she'd married, but she was more than ready to settle down in one place and start over.

It's why she accepted the principal's job and was moving to Hallbrook. Having her brother around would make things easier with Gabby. Even now, he was a huge help and keeping her daughter while she completed the sale of the house and closed out all aspects of her life in Boston. When the closing on the house had gotten moved up a few days, it had been a relief, but it didn't change all the other things she needed to get done.

After stopping at the house for a few last-minute outdoor hanging planters, Lynette drove away for the last time without so much as a glance in the rearview mirror. She headed to the motel where she'd registered to stay for the next two nights. Bingo would be happy to see her after being left in the room while she ran errands, but Lynette had known the attorney wouldn't have appreciated it if she'd brought the dog to his office. And she hadn't wanted to overload Keith by asking him to watch Gabby *and* the dog, the two a handful at times. Not to mention, Bingo kept Lynette company.

She pushed open the door and was greeted by a happy-go-lucky canine. The dog wasn't used to being cooped up, and she grabbed his leash and headed back outside to let him take care of his business and get some fresh air.

It was a short walk, Lynette wanting nothing more than to settle back in the plush armchair, a cup of tea in hand. Bingo came over, laying down and placing her head across Lynette's foot, his eyes watching her every move.

She raised her cup in the air. "To new beginnings. Calm, stable, beginnings," she corrected. Taking a sip, she let out a deep breath and started to make a mental checklist of what needed to be done before she could leave. She missed Gabby, and the early closing would allow her to get back to her daughter sooner than expected.

Gabby had become withdrawn after the death of her father and was now struggling with even more change. Keith would look after her, but Lynette wanted to be there for her daughter. A calming, stable force in her life. The same words describing what they both craved.

Lynette pulled out her phone from the dark depths of her oversized handbag. She was surprised to see she'd missed a call from Keith, but then she'd put it on silent for the closing, so it made sense. Noticing the voice mail icon was lit, she cued up the keypad and press play.

Hey sis. Had a plant emergency in Pennsylvania and had to fly out. Gabby's staying with my neighbor and good friend, Connor Weston until you get there. He's a great guy with a twelve-year-old son, and they were going camping up at White Mountain State Park this weekend. He agreed to take Gabby along. She'll have a blast. Call me when you get a chance.

Lynette jumped to her feet, sloshing tea down the front of the blouse. *Was her brother out of his mind?* How could he do such a thing? Sending her daughter off with a stranger was beyond all realm of stupidity. She thought she knew her brother better than this. It didn't matter if the guy wasn't a stranger to Keith; he was a stranger to Lynette. *And Gabby.*

Would she ever be free of chaos? First Dirk, and now her brother. When would it stop? Lynette called Keith, growing angrier by the second when he didn't answer. Making a quick decision, she started throwing her things together in the suitcase she had only just unpacked. There was no way she was going to sit here and do nothing, her maternal instinct kicking in and wanting to make sure Gabby was okay.

"Come on, Bingo. We've got to go get Gabby." The dog jumped to his feet, eager to go do whatever it was Lynette wanted, as long as she didn't leave him behind. Bingo had been a rescue dog and had separation anxiety, which was another reason she hadn't let her brother keep him while she finished up in Boston. With his brown and white coloring, medium size, and floppy ears, they weren't sure what mixed breed he was—other than a super cute, soft, and cuddly one.

The rest of her errands would have to wait.

At least she knew where this guy Connor was headed, and it wouldn't be hard to find White

Mountain State Park. The hardest part would be finding them once she got there.

Chapter Two

♥

LYNETTE WOKE TO THE sound of her alarm. Her calls to Gabby had gone unanswered, which only made her more anxious for her daughter's safety. Logically, she knew her brother wouldn't trust the guy unless he was trustworthy, but the other side of her brain was terrified of anything going wrong. She'd already lost her husband, and Gabby was her lifeline through all the changes.

Arriving late in the evening, her way into the state park had been barred. When she'd finally gotten through to her brother, he'd reassured her all would be okay and, of course, tried to tease her about her over-the-top reaction. She didn't see it that way, but it was why she finally relented and had spent the night at Keith's. The park gates opened at eight A.M., and Lynette planned on being there.

Bingo hopped in the car, and they made their way through the winding road out of town. She didn't have to wait long for the gates to open. Pulling up to the registration booth, she rolled down her window, hoping the attendant would be able to help her find the Weston's campsite.

"Good morning. Checking in?" the young woman asked, a concerned expression on her face.

"No. I'm here to pick up my daughter," Lynette said.

"Do you know what site she's on? I can write you a temporary pass, but you might not want to linger. They are setting up checkpoints this morning to warn everyone about the rising river waters. It looks as though the road could flood. If that happens, people will get stuck on whichever side they're on."

"I saw the work trucks as I drove in. When do they expect the floodwaters to cover the road?" she asked, more than a little concerned.

"Oh, probably not for at least another twen-ty-four hours, so you should be fine. We're just trying to warn everyone ahead of time."

"I see. Well, that's good news. As to the campsite, I don't know the number. I was hoping you could help me figure out where she is. The thing is she's staying with my brother's friend, and I arrived back at Hallbrook early so I could pick her up," Lynette said, trying to appeal to the young woman's helpful side.

The woman shook her head. "*Ummm*, I'm sorry. It's part of our privacy policy, and we don't give out that kind of information. You would need to know who you're visiting, or be staying here, or get a day pass to visit."

"I know who he is if that helps. His name is Connor Weston. I've tried calling his phone, but no one is answering." Lynette said a little prayer, hoping the woman would see her way to supplying the site number.

"The cell service here is pretty bad, so it's not surprising. Let me see if I can locate someone by that name." The woman clicked away at the keys of her computer, nodded, and then looked back at Lynette. "Yes, I've got him right here. He's in site D33." She handed Lynette a map of the campground.

"Thank you so much," Lynette said, feeling relieved.

"I'll write you a day pass. Will that give you plenty of time?"

"Good heavens, yes. I won't be here long." Only long enough to get Gabby and get out. At least the rising waters wouldn't pose a problem for her, but it was a good thing she'd come when she did.

The attendant filled out a pass and handed it to Lynette. "Have a nice day and enjoy your time here. I've circled the site on the map, and it shows you how to get there. Otherwise, just follow the signs."

"Thank you." Lynette moved forward, glancing at the map before tossing it on the front seat. "I think we should follow the signs, boy. What do you think?" she asked the dog, patting him on the head. "I mean, how hard can it be?" As a non-camper, she hoped they weren't famous last words.

The speed limit was fifteen, but she found herself pushing twenty, tapping her brakes to slow down when the dial crept up to twenty-five. A small sign on the right announced A – D should turn left, and E — G should go straight ahead. Unfortunately, the time it took to read the sign had her already past the turn. She did a U-turn, and made a right, going slower this time.

Lynette passed the first two loop entrances and finally came to the D loop. Going through the gates, she followed the road around, the speed limit now ten, making it easy for her to check the site numbers. Coming to number thirty-three, she pulled in behind the truck parked there.

She let Bingo out of the car, the dog running around to check out all the new smells. There was one large tent but no sign of anyone awake yet. Lynette had always pictured campers up at dawn, but apparently, she was wrong.

Unsure of what to do, she hesitated. In the end, the morning chill made the decision for her.

"Yoo-hoo. Hello," she called out lamely, hoping Gabby would recognize her voice, or this Connor guy would be awake enough to get out of his warm sleeping bag and come talk to her.

What she didn't expect, however, was no response. "Hello," she called out again. "Anyone here?" Still no answer. Indecision gave her just enough time to decide her next move. It was her daughter, and she had every right. Lynette started to unzip the tent flap, hesitating only a moment.

What if she had the wrong site?

This could go horribly wrong. Gabby was more than enough reason for her to continue. She pushed back the flap to peer inside, surprised to find it empty. Three sleeping bags, but none occupied.

Lynette let out a sigh, unsure if in relief or trepidation. They must have gotten up early and were already out doing whatever it was people did when they camped. With no clue where they'd gone, she wasn't sure where to look, but sitting here wasn't a part of her plan. "Bingo, get in the car. Let's drive around the loop and see if we can spot them."

Three times around the loop and nothing. Left with no choice, she returned to the campsite to wait them out. Glancing at her phone, she confirmed there was still no cell service. Calling her daughter fourteen times wouldn't change a thing, but it would worry her daughter if she did get service and the missed-call alerts came rolling in. Gabby had enough stress and worries without Lynette adding to them.

An hour later, Lynette got out of the car. She put the leash on Bingo and opted to take a walk around the loop. She had to do something. Sitting around only managed to key her up more, her frazzled nerves nearing the end of what they could take.

As they neared the campsite again, Bingo suddenly pulled at his leash, the surprise move costing Lynette her grip on the handle. The dog took off running and headed straight for the site, cutting through the woods. "Bingo! Come back," she hollered.

Lynette cut through the woods to follow, slowing when she spotted his destination. The sight of Bingo and Gabby hugging warmed her heart and released the tightly held tension she'd been carrying around ever since she found out her daughter was camping.

Thank you, Lord.

She stepped into the cleared area of the campsite, as three confused faces turned to look over at her.

"Mom, what are you doing here?" Gabby was the first to speak as she crossed the campsite and came to hug Lynette. "I saw the car and couldn't believe it." She reached down to rub Bingo behind his ears.

"I came to get you. Your Uncle Keith told me what happened, and I, ummm," she said, letting her words trail off as she glanced at the man headed her way. Tall, athletic build, and decidedly handsome, his ball cap proclaiming a love for the Red Sox. "I didn't think you'd want to camp. It's not really your thing." It wasn't Lynette's thing for sure, and it was a far cry better of an excuse than the truth—that she didn't trust Connor. Saying it to his face didn't seem like a smart move and would be rude given the situation.

Gabby let out a huge sign. "I wouldn't know if it's my thing since I've never done it. You didn't need to come get me."

The man reached out to shake hands. "Hi, I'm Connor Weston. You must be Lynette Taylor."

His grip was firm and strong, a trait she had always admired in people. "I am. Sorry to arrive unannounced, but I came to pick up my daughter. Keith should have let me know first that he was called out of town. If he had, I would have been here sooner, and we wouldn't have intruded on your father-son outing."

"It was fine. Gabby seems to be enjoying herself. Even caught a few fish this morning." The man's warm smile and blue eyes held a note of kindness she couldn't ignore. Seeing him face-to-face dispelled her initial fears about the man. She should have trusted her brother more, but still, it was her daughter.

"Fishing?" She glanced at Gabby for confirmation. "*You* willingly got up early and crawled out of the tent to go fishing? *Hello*. Where is my daughter?" Lynette teased. Gabby would sleep to noon on days she didn't have to wake up for school. Which come Monday morning, she'd start back in Hallbrook and finish out the year.

Gabby shrugged. "It was cool. Connor, errr, Mr. Weston taught me how to throw in a line." Her daughter shot a glance at the man. "I mean, it was okay and all. I could have done it without his help, but you know, it made him feel helpful, I guess."

It was an interesting change in attitude, one Lynette would have like to explore more. They could talk about it over pizza tonight. "I'm glad you learned something new. Now, why don't you go get your things, and we can be out of Mr. Weston's hair. We need to get a move on in case the waters on the river rise quicker than expected."

Gabby shook her head. "But I don't want to go. If you had called, I could have told you that." Her daughter scratched behind the dog's ears as he sat patiently beside her.

"I tried. There's no cell service." Lynette hadn't expected any resistance from her daughter. Gratitude had been more on the menu the way she saw it. "Now that I'm here, we should go, and this isn't up for discussion. They've been issuing warnings all morning, and I've already had to wait a couple of hours for you to return. We need to leave. Now." Lynette hadn't wanted to play the strong parent hand in front of the others, but her daughter was leaving her no choice.

"The rangers stopped by this morning and dropped off a flyer to warn us about the potential river flooding. They're hoping it won't crest the dam and only mild flooding on the roads will occur," Connor said.

"Which is why we decided to stay," Gabby interjected. "We are fine."

The boy by the campfire looked up, a scowl on his face, but quickly returned his attention to moving some of the logs around.

"She's welcome to stay. Honestly, she's no trouble at all," Connor said, taking her daughter's side. Except Lynette had come all this way, and she wasn't leaving without Gabby. And she didn't appreciate his offer since it would only make things worse.

"That's nice of you, but it's not an option. We have so much to do, and now that I'm here, Gabby and I need to get settled." It all sounded plausible, at least to Lynette.

Gabby, not so much. She stood there, arms crossed in defiance. "I want to stay, Mom. I never get to do anything I want to do." Now wasn't the time for her daughter to act out, something she was quick to do lately when she didn't get her way.

"Sorry, sweetheart, maybe another time. Let's go."

"Fine, but just for the record, I was having fun. Something I haven't had in a while."

Lynette bit back the words she wanted to say. This was a discussion best had in private. "We need to buy school supplies."

"School's boring. And there are only four weeks left anyway. Seems pretty dumb to start a new school if you ask me." Gabby spoke loud enough to be heard but headed for the tent to do as she was told. Her daughter was laying on the guilt thick, but it wasn't anything Lynette couldn't handle.

Lynette said a quick prayer for patience, needing the extra strength to get through this next challenge. It was always something with Gabby. "With me starting the new job Monday, you have to go to school. You're not old enough to stay home alone, and you know it."

"Yeah, pipsqueak, you need a babysitter," the boy said as her daughter passed by him.

"Grow up," Gabby said, taking a chip out of her bag and tossing it at the kid.

"I'm sorry about all this," Lynette said, trying to apologize for her daughter's behavior.

"You really are welcome to let her stay, now that you know I'm not an ax murderer," Connor said. Like father, like son, getting in their digs. In Lynette's experience, it was a sign of insecurity. His son, she understood, given all that Keith had told her. Connor, not so much.

But it wasn't her problem. Her problem was to move forward with a safe, structured, non-chaotic future with Gabby. "Thanks, but it's all good."

"I understand. Maybe some other time."

"Sure thing." *Not.* "Bingo, let's go." Gabby came out of the tent and headed her way. "Thank Mr. Weston for allowing you to tag along," Lynette said, trying to wrap it up and leave.

"Yes, Mother," Gabby said, her tone coming across loud and clear as unhappy with being over-ridden and Connor's offer nixed. "Thanks, Mr. Weston. Bye, Trey. At least with me leaving, neither one of you will have any competition catching fish." Verbal digs were on the menu today, her daughter falling in line with the others.

"You're welcome, and I resent that," Connor said with a wink.

"She's right, Dad. You haven't caught a thing," Trey said, stirring up the fire with a stick.

Connor chuckled. "My luck's about to change. Besides, I'm blaming my bad morning on the rushing river water. It's not easy keeping up with my line, *and* helping the two of you fish," he said, trying to tease his son.

"In your dreams," Trey retorted.

Gabby looked from Trey to Connor, her expression darkening. "Let's go, Mom." Lynette wasn't sure what set off the sullen expression, but whatever it was, Gabby wasn't likely to share on the ride back to town.

Chapter Three

♥

CONNOR SENT THEM ONE last wave as Lynette backed out of the site. She followed the signs out of the state park and back to Hallbrook. They passed a scenic lookout five minutes later, and Gabby had yet to say a word. The twenty-minute drive would seem like hours at this point. Even Bingo sensed the tension and lay curled up on the back seat, blissfully sleeping through it all.

Rounding the next curve, a flurry of activity suddenly appeared in front of her on the road. Police car lights were flashing, cones had been put out, and several officers were standing around talking.

"What's going on, Mom?" Gabby asked, breaking her vow of silence.

"No idea, but I reckon we're about to find out." She drew to a stop as the police officer flagged her down. Opening her window, she looked at him expectantly.

Woof. Woof. Bingo went into protective mode and made his presence known.

"Hush, Bingo. It's okay," Lynette said, hoping to settle him down.

The tall, dark-haired officer stepped closer, a quick glance to the back seat and at the dog. "Good afternoon, ma'am. The road's closed, and you'll need to turn around."

It took Lynette a second to grasp what he was saying. "Closed? What do you mean? And turn around and go where?" This wasn't supposed to happen. The woman had said she would have hours to get Gabby before there was any real concern.

"The river dam broke with all the heavy rain we had the past few days. The water has flooded the road, and it's impassable. As to back where? That would be back to the state park. Where you came from." His matter of fact, stoic attitude did little to help her process the news.

"I can't go back. I don't have a place to stay. I was just picking up my daughter."

"Sorry, there's nothing we can do."

When would anything go right? Or easy? "How long till the road reopens? We can wait here, I guess," Lynette said, resigning herself to a long wait in the car with a daughter not even talking to her.

"There's no way to know. The water is still rising as the rainfall drains down from the mountains. It could be a few days before this road is reopened. At least whatever site you were staying on is yours for the duration since no one's getting in either," the ranger offered. He thought the information helpful, but he couldn't be more wrong.

"I can't believe this." Lynette shook her head.

Her daughter, on the other hand, brightened. "This means we need to go back to the camp for the rest of the weekend. It sounds good to me." Mother Nature was clearly on her daughter's side but mocking Lynette.

She'd had enough of the great outdoors.

Lynette closed her eyes and let out a deep sigh. "Guess we don't have any choice." She reopened them, hoping it was all a nightmare—no such luck.

"No, ma'am, you don't." The officer stepped back and waved her through to allow the turn around.

Lynette rolled the window up. "Don't say anything," she said, not wanting to hear Gabby gloat about getting her way. But her daughter's attitude was something Lynette needed to consider. Gabby, who hadn't found much to cheer about lately, was on board with this whole camping thing. For her daughter, she'd do this. Okay, so it's not like she had a choice in the matter.

It wasn't long before she stopped at the registration booth, thinking she would need a new pass. A sign on the front door announced that due to the road closure, the office was closed. The ranger's contact information was listed in case of an emergency. She headed for site D33, knowing her way this time. Pulling in, Gabby bounded out of the car, Bingo hot on her heels.

"Guess what?" Gabby called out as the guys headed her way. "You're stuck with us, whether you like it or not."

"What's going on?" Connor asked. "Not that it's a problem, but what changed your mind?"

"Mother Nature at her worst," Lynette exclaimed, joining the others. "The dam broke, and now, the road out of here is closed."

"Good grief, just when I thought we got rid of them." Trey shook his head and returned to the fire.

"This ought to be interesting," Connor said, stroking his chin.

"What?" she asked.

"Well, I'll need to put up the other tent for starters. We can't all fit in one. I'm sure we can figure something out with the bedding. We can do boys in one tent and girls in the other. It's a good thing I already had another tent packed when we added Gabby to the group. We'd be like sardines in a can otherwise." Connor smiled and headed for the truck.

"Lucky us." At least if she was stuck here, she had a private place to sleep. It would have been uncomfortable no matter what the situation to be in the same tent with strangers, emergency or otherwise. "You said for starters, what else am I not going to like?" she asked, following him.

"The food situation. I only planned for three people, not four. I sure hope you like freshly caught catfish. It was on the menu for breakfast and dinner, but now it may be more than that." Connor shot her a wink, but she wasn't sure he was teasing.

Lynette scrunched up her face, the idea not one of her choosing. She might have to go hungry. "I'll pass. Snacks are fine by me."

"I'm with Mom on this," Gabby declared. At least they were back on the same team.

"Girls. What sissies," Trey called out. "More for me, I reckon."

"That should make you happy," Gabby snapped back.

"Mind your own business, pipsqueak."

"Knock it off, you two. It looks like we're going to be spending more time together. It'd be a whole lot more fun if everyone got along."

"Fun would have been if they weren't here, but whatever." Trey, it seemed, could be just as moody as Gabby. Together, it was a lot to deal with.

"Trey..." Connor wasn't cutting the kid any slack, much the same way she didn't put up with her daughter acting out either.

"Fine. Sorry. Let's all go have a merry time, like one big happy family." His sarcastic words were a stark reminder of her and Gabby's past.

A *happy family* wasn't something she could remember since Gabby turned five and started school. Then multiple schools became the norm, each move becoming increasingly difficult. They'd even talked about Dirk getting out of the military, but now, he'd never get the chance. Lynette glanced at her daughter, only to find her on the verge of tears. Gabby turned and ran into the woods, Bingo hot on her heels.

"You stepped right into that one, son. I reckon you need to go after her and fix it," Connor said, watching as Gabby disappeared.

"Girls," Trey mumbled, shuffling off into the woods. The fact he did what he was told on the first go-round was a sign he was a good kid. And good parenting.

"Sorry. He didn't mean anything by what he said, but it was a stupid comment to make. He meant it more about his own family, forgetting other families had their own share of problems."

"I know. I'm sorry we're ruining your father-son weekend." Too late, Lynette remembered they were dealing with some broken-family issues of their own.

Connor shook his head, admiring Lynette's compassion and understanding. The woman had just been stranded camping with strangers, and she was holding her own, trying to make the best of it. "You're not. Going with the flow and dealing with change is all part of life. I'm used to it, or I was anyway. Hopefully soon, I'll be back on the road, and life will get interesting again."

"Boring sounds pretty good to me right now," Lynette said, her gaze never straying from the wooded area where her daughter had run off.

"We'll have to see what we can do to change your mind, starting with the catfish. You need to live dangerously and try new food," he teased, not even sure *he* could stomach catfish for breakfast. Bacon and eggs sounded far better.

"I'll pass," Lynette said, her face scrunched up, reminding him of Gabby.

"Say that after I cook it and your mouth starts to water." Connor laughed, moving back to the fireplace, watching as the kids came back to the campsite, Bingo right beside them. He was better at this parenting thing than he gave himself credit for, but in some areas, he needed a little prodding.

"Happy? I'm back. Now can we go do something? Sitting around here is boring with a capital B," Gabby said, kicking at the dirt.

"Sure enough. How about a hike up to the lake for more fishing after breakfast?" Connor asked, trying to keep the peace and bring the high emotions down a notch or two.

"I can't believe this. First, we get stuck with one girl; now we've got to deal with two. When will the nightmare end?" Trey asked, but this time, he cracked a grin. Whether he meant to tease or not, it had come out that way, which was a far sight better than when he'd taken off after Gabby.

"You're just sore because Gabby caught more fish than you did this morning." He shot a wink at Lynette, admiring the soft curve of her cheekbones, flushed with the fresh air.

Trey shook his head. "I'm taking a walk around the loop. Alone, if that's okay with you," he said, an unhappy expression on his face.

A walk would do him some good. Or, at least, Connor hoped so. "Fine. Once around the loop and then back to check-in." He was all for giving his son some freedom but doing it safely was still in order. Trey walked away, his steps closer to stomping in anger.

"I'm sorry, Connor. We've ruined everything for him. It sounds like he really needed some breathing space out here with you."

"No, I'm sorry for his attitude and manners. He'll get over it. Let's get some breakfast. We have fresh fish..."

Gabby looked up, shocked, her expression mirroring Lynette's.

"No way," they both said in unison.

"You weren't serious?" Lynette asked.

"Just kidding." Connor grinned back at the two of them. "That's for supper. Trust me, catfish in tinfoil with lemon and butter over the campfire is a killer meal." It was one of his favorites when they camped, something they didn't do often enough.

"If you say so, Mr. Weston. But don't expect me to clean any of them. I did the catching." Gabby, it would seem, would come around to the idea for supper. More proof it wouldn't be long before he turned her into a real camper. Lynette, he was still on the undecided side of how that would work out, but he wouldn't stop trying. She might be stuck here a few days and it would go far easier if they enjoyed the outdoor experience.

"True enough, young lady," he said, earning a grin.

"Can I take a walk around the loop?" Gabby asked.

Connor nodded. "Yes, but the same rules apply we gave Trey."

"No," Lynette chimed in, reversing the decision, earning her another of Gabby's defiant looks.

"Why not?" she asked.

"Because you're eleven, and you're a girl, and there are too many dangers." Lynette was a worrywart; that much was clear. But then, that was the difference between having a son and a daughter.

Connor wasn't sure it was his place to interject, but he couldn't help but try. As a boy, he remembered all too clearly how restrictive it felt to be on a tight leash. "It's a campground, and it's safe. She'll be fine."

"How do you know?" Lynette asked, doubt in her voice.

"I've been coming here all my life. The campers who visit are good people. Outdoor people communing with nature." It was true, although anywhere you went, there was possible danger. You couldn't let fear control your life, or it would control you.

"But there's no guarantee," Lynette said, shaking her head. "I need a guarantee," her strained voice was on the verge of cracking. There was something deeper going on here, and Connor was only just beginning to put two and two together.

"This isn't fair," Gabby fumed.

"Please try to see this my way, Gabby. This is exactly why I came here in the first place. To keep you safe," she said, pleading with her daughter to understand.

Connor shot her a look as he shook his head. It was no more than he'd expected when she arrived this morning, ready to take up the gauntlet and escort her daughter home. "I wondered."

"About?" she asked.

"Your true motive for showing up," Connor said, not pulling any punches.

Hands on hips, Lynette glared. "Wonder all you want—it's my daughter."

"That's true." Connor walked away, stopping at the picnic table.

"I'm not a baby," Gabby said, her words clear even from a distance. Lynette was right, it wasn't his daughter, and he needed to butt out.

"Then quit acting like one."

"Fine." Her daughter stormed over to the fireplace, grabbing up the poker stick to act as fire attendant in Trey's absence. Bingo took up residence next to her as he curled up on the ground.

It was on the tip of his tongue to warn Gabby to be careful and inform her of the dangers associated with a campfire, but given all that had gone on, he kept his mouth shut. They needed some breakfast, and it was his job to make sure they were all fed.

Chapter Four

♥

LYNETTE TAYLOR WAS AS prickly as they came, especially when it involved her daughter. There was a possibility that she had a good point about Gabby being too young to walk alone. It's just that he was used to Trey. Her reversal of his decision confirmed the real reason she'd shown up, the truth stinging a bit as he realized he couldn't be trusted to watch her daughter.

Baseball was the same thing. His whole life, he just wasn't good enough. Not for his dad, not for his ex-wife, not for the major leagues, and now, not for Lynette. He couldn't do a thing about three of those. But he could train harder, push himself to the max, and give the minors one last chance to take him back—and then go for the gold with the majors. It was all he'd ever wanted, and at his age, the dream was fast becoming a thing of the past.

He pulled apart the bacon strips and tossed them into the frying pan. A simple breakfast was in order considering his extra guest. Gabby went back in the tent while he cooked, ignoring the adults. Her attitude changes were a bit confusing, but Connor was sure it had something to do with her father. He'd noticed it from the beginning, her on-again, off-again attitude toward him. It's like she wanted to join in but didn't want Connor to know she liked it–or his help.

"What can I do?" Lynette asked, coming to stand next to him.

Trey wasn't one to voluntarily chip in, so it was a nice change for her to offer. "I don't start the eggs cooking until the bacon's done, and the bread doesn't get toasted until the eggs are cooking." He grinned. "But if you could set the table, it would be a big help."

"And how do you propose to cook the toast?" Lynette glanced at the fireplace and then back at him as he placed the skillet on the grill, centering it over the flames.

"On a stick." Connor focused his attention on the bacon, unable to wipe the smirk from his face. "The old-fashioned campfire way. You know, pioneer style."

"Seriously? Like one at a time. Yuk. Sounds like a recipe for smoke-flamed bread." Her face was scrunched up in distaste, the idea of blackened toast not appealing.

"It's actually not bad if done right." Connor chuckled. "But no, I'm not serious. I have a toaster in the black box over there," he said, pointing next to the tent. "And you can plug it in at the table next to the power box over there," he added, pointing in the direction of the electrical post. He enjoyed camping, but he also enjoyed some of the modern conveniences campgrounds offered. Electricity and water were at the top of his list.

"Very funny." Lynette rolled her eyes, clearly not amused by his teasing. She started to lay out the paper plates and plastic utensils, carefully folding a napkin to put under each fork. It was almost comical since it's not like they were eating a fancy dinner or anything.

With the table set, she joined him at the fire and held her hands out toward the glowing embers to warm them. "I hate that Gabby's in a snit over this. And I'm sorry if I came across as rude. I'm grateful you helped Keith out in a pinch."

"It's okay, I get it. You had every right to be worried. I'm not good at this parenting thing, clearly. It was one of my ex-wife's chief complaints." One of many, but he wasn't going to bore Lynette with the details.

"Oh? I would have thought by now, you would be an expert. Trey is about twelve or thirteen, isn't he?"

"Twelve. But no. His mother took care of him for the most part while I was away traveling on the road. I play baseball, or at least I did until I was injured. It's only this past year I've done the full-time parenting role, and it's when my ex split town. It's not been easy for Trey since the divorce." It hadn't been easy for either one of them. Disillusioned in life, they both had some hurdles to clear.

"I didn't realize you were divorced. I'm sorry. Keith mentioned you played baseball. What kind of travel team were you on?"

Connor laughed. It wasn't often he ran into someone he had to explain his life to. "I played college ball on a scholarship and was drafted into the minors. There's a lot of travel to games all over the country. Darlene, my ex, didn't approve of the way things turned out when I was injured, and any real shot at the majors vanished." He'd known they weren't on the same page about a lot of things, but it had never crossed his mind she'd leave him. But then, her new boyfriend played in the majors for the Texans. While his dream faded, her dream of being a major league player's wife was close to becoming a reality judging by the last text he received from her.

"I see. Unfortunately, I understand her reasoning. Dirk, my husband, constantly had us on the move with changing bases and deployments. It was quite exhausting raising Gabby alone, or so it seemed like it was alone anyway."

Connor had heard similar remarks from Darlene and then some. It wasn't just the time he was away, though. For his ex, it had been the need for social parties and upward movement. The right connections. She wanted to move into high society, and

Connor hadn't delivered. It's not to say he couldn't have handled things better, but Darlene hadn't minded the being alone part as much as she minded the failure part. "I'm sorry about your husband. Keith told me what happened."

Lynette looked down at the fire, watching the dancing flames with sudden interest. "Thank you. It was a little over a year ago. It took me this long to pick up the pieces and figure out what to do next, which is why the move to Hallbrook. Starting over. What kind of injury? Do you still play?" Lynette asked, clearly trying to shift the conversation back to him.

"I threw out my shoulder. The extent of the injury caused me to have surgery, which in turn meant a longer recovery. That's when Darlene left, and I became a full-time dad with a bum shoulder. I had to quit the minors. My shoulder's better now, and I think I'm ready to jump back in the action when the Red Sox minor leagues hold tryouts."

"But what about Trey?" Lynette asked, her voice soft but with a tinge of disapproval.

Connor knew what she was asking. "He can do remote learning and travel with me. It's the best of both worlds. He can see me play, learn the practice routine and commitment, and get an edge toward playing ball at a higher level than school baseball. Trey needs to get more involved and be seen by scouts. I can do that for him if I get back into the minors." He had high aspirations for Trey and opening doors was the best thing he could do for his son.

"Children need stability, and what you're suggesting would be total chaos. Trust me, I've lived with chaos for ten years, and both Gabby and I crave a feeling of belonging somewhere. Settling down. Making long-term friends. Have you talked to Trey about this?"

"My son is different than most kids. I think he wants to see me succeed. Have a dad he can respect. And he wants to be the best he can be in baseball. Chip off the old block if you ask me."

"We'll have to agree to disagree on that one. From what little I've seen already, I think he would rather have you around more often. What boy doesn't want his father to spend time with him? He seemed upset to have this father-son camping trip ruined."

"Like you said, we can agree to disagree." He knew his son and what was best for him. Connor's own father had been disappointed when he wasn't selected for the little league team he'd tried out for when he was nine. It had pushed Connor to try harder, and he'd succeeded by most people's standards—just not some. Not that it changed the outcome. His father had still walked away from the family. And any success Connor achieved was never enough, his efforts always falling short of the old man's expectations. Connor knew it was his job to show his son how to persevere to the finish and help him along the way. Something his own father hadn't done for him.

Lynette simply didn't understand.

He finished cooking the bacon and moved them to a paper plate covered with extra paper towels to absorb the grease. Connor looked up as Trey walked back into the campsite. "Hey there. Breakfast is almost ready. Can you do me a favor and take Gabby for a quick walk around the loop with Bingo? Provided her mother says it's okay, that is."

Lynette frowned and let out a deep sigh. "I'm not overprotective. Or not much. A walk is fine, but don't feel you have to, Trey. She'll be okay."

His son plopped into a nearby chair. "Good, I don't need to babysit a girl," he said, rolling his eyes to emphasize the point.

"It's not babysitting," Gabby said, coming out of the tent. "I'm too old for a babysitter. Get over yourself. I just wanted the same chance to check out the place. I'm not the one who says I can't go alone." She crossed her arms in defiance.

"Trey..." Connor shot him one of his do-the-right-thing looks.

"Fine. It's not like it seems to matter what I want." Connor knew he was talking about his mother and the entire situation, not just the camping trip. He wouldn't push the issue considering his son had just agreed to take a walk with Gabby.

"Thanks. Make it quick; it won't take long for the eggs," Connor said. If Trey had his way, it would be closer to a jog around the loop.

The two of them walked away, Gabby holding Bingo's leash. It would do them good, and might even help them work out whatever issues they had with each other. If Gabby was going to be at Keith's a lot, they'd be seeing way more of each other than either one wanted at this point. The same went for him and Lynette, but as adults, they would find a way to get along, even if they weren't on the same page about much of anything.

Connor Weston and his son were interesting characters. One was overtly opinionated, and the other overtly antagonistic and opinionated. Given the situation, Lynette assumed Trey had a lot of resentment he was dealing with. It was something he had in common with Gabby, so it was a shame they didn't see eye to eye.

Connor, on the other hand, was way full of himself. Attractive, yes. Down to earth, absolutely not. The total opposite of what Lynette wanted for Gabby. The sooner this little outing ended, the better as far as she was concerned.

"I'll start the toast if I have your approval," she teased, holding up the loaf of bread.

"Very funny, but yes, it's time. Unless you want cold eggs and bacon." Connor cracked the eggs into the pan. He watched her closely as she manned the toaster, buttered each finished piece, and covered them with a napkin. It was as though he hadn't trusted her to do the job correctly.

By the time the eggs were done, the kids had returned, Bingo leading the way. Both must have been super hungry because they washed up and sat at the picnic table almost immediately. Trey chose the seat at the far opposite end from Gabby, but still, they were at the same table.

The kids reached for the marmalade at the same time. Trey glared at Gabby before releasing his hold and letting her have the jar. The kid had good manners.

"Breakfast is ready," Connor said, delivering the eggs to each plate. "Lynette, if you could take some bacon and pass it around, that would be great. And kids, remember there are four of us eating, so take your portion accordingly." Connor chuckled. "I'm sure you two can do the math."

Neither one answered, but they were told and dug into their breakfast without a word. Bingo, on the other hand, made his hungry status known as he went around the table, nudging elbows and trying to beg food.

"Bingo, go lie down," Lynette ordered, not wanting him to get bad habits. He slunk off toward the fireplace. "What am I going to do for dog food?" she questioned, hoping Connor had answers. He'd already mentioned a food shortage, not that she wanted Bingo eating people food.

"We could always ask some of the other campers. I'm sure they'd be more than willing to share given the circumstances."

It was something she should have thought of herself, the answer simple enough. And it was an excellent solution, not that she liked the idea of going door to door asking. It would be a good job for Gabby and Trey to do together—something to expedite a friendship of sorts. "Kids? Any takers to find some doge food," she asked.

Connor glared at his son. "You know, for however long we are going to be here together, it's going to be miserable if we all can't get along." He turned to Lynette for support, smiling at her when she nodded her encouragement. It was as though they were on the same page, which was odd considering they weren't five minutes ago.

"It's not me; it's her. She's always asking questions and wanting to tag along. I shouldn't have to babysit her," Trey rattled off all his complaints.

"And I told you, it's not babysitting. It's two kids hanging out because we happen to want to do the same thing. So sue me because I liked fishing. Or is it because I caught more than you and you're jealous?" Gabby wasn't backing down.

Trey snickered. "Jealous of a girl. Hah! That'll be the day. All girls are the same. And then they grow up to be women and nothing changes. More of us guys should learn our lesson and steer clear." He took a bite of food and half turned away as if it would make a difference.

"Yup. Jealous," Gabby added with satisfaction. Her daughter was pushing all the boy's hot buttons. It wasn't like her, and Lynette was more than a little confused by her attitude.

Connor's jaw was clenched tight, his tension mounting. "Okay, you two, this isn't what I had in mind."

Lynette reached for Gabby's arm. "Gabby, honey, dial it back, please. We are their guests. It's nice of them to help us out. Otherwise, we'd be eating fish for breakfast, lunch, and dinner, provided you could catch more. Oh, and clean and cook them." Her lips curved into a smile as she leaned over to bump her daughter's shoulder.

"No way. We'd go hungry first. Besides, it's not me. Trey is just being a bore. Most boys his age are."

"Am not," Trey said in defense.

"Are too," Gabby retorted."

So asking them to find dog food together wasn't such a good idea. Separate campsites for the duration of their stay sounded more reasonable.

Connor stood, taking his plate with him. "Stop. I tell you what—I'm going to trade places with Lynette, and you two are going to sit next to each other. And if you want to speak, say something nice. Otherwise, I want silence. And if you can't get along, there's no way we're going to hike up to the lake and fish some more. We can sit right here and be bored."

Gabby's eyes lit up briefly and then became shuttered, leaving Lynette to wonder what was really going on. "Works for me."

Was it possible her daughter was looking to bond with Connor? She'd been so reserved this past year, and it was as though Lynette was watching a sideshow of her daughter's reawakening. Gabby stood, moving to the other side of the table. She sat at the far end, her back slightly to Trey. Giving in and yet holding her own. It wouldn't do to have her get attached to hanging around Connor for any reason. When they left here, they'd hardly ever see him again if she had anything to say about it.

Lynette swatted away a fly that had joined the breakfast affair. And then another. "Who invited these pesky flies to breakfast?" she asked, irritated at having to compete for her food. Food that, in all honesty, was far tastier than she'd expected. Who knew bacon and eggs cooked over a fire could taste this good?

Connor laughed. "It's called the great outdoors." He finished off his breakfast, stood, and took his plate to the fire, tossing it in. "Think of it as an open invitation to all. At least they don't eat much."

"I see. But you're not talking about wild animals or anything when you say *all*. Right?" she asked, just to be on the safe side.

"Just a bear or two," Trey said, a smirk on his face.

Gabby turned back to the group. "Or maybe even a cougar," she added. The two kids glanced at each other and then looked away, leaving Lynette to wonder what they were up to.

"You aren't serious. It's a joke, right?" she asked.

Connor came back to the picnic table and stood next to Trey. "We definitely have bears and cougars here. This is a national forest and plenty of wildlife. But don't let it worry you none. The bears only come around for food which is why we put everything up out of reach and out of scent," he said, his grin much like the children's.

Adrenaline raced through her body, fear driving it from head to toe. This wasn't something she'd considered when she first found out she had no choice but to camp. "But what about the cougars?" Lynette asked, more than a little concerned.

"One time, I saw it on a show that if you tap two sticks together when you're in the woods, it keeps the cougars away," Gabby said without so much as a hint of a smile.

"She's right," Trey added. His words sent a chill down Lynette's spine.

"Don't worry, I'll protect you on our hike to the lake," Connor said, equally serious.

"By the sounds of it, I should be able to take care of myself. Thanks anyway," Lynette said, picking up her plate to take it to the fire.

The three of them burst out laughing the second she turned her back.

She spun back around. "What's so funny? Are you teasing?"

"I'm not. I really did see a show once where they did that," Gabby said with a straight face.

Lynette couldn't tell if they were all having fun at her expense or not, but she'd find out soon enough on their hike. If the others tapped sticks together to ward off the cougars, she'd know they were serious. Between the flies, the critters, and the whims of Mother Nature, she couldn't understand why anyone would want to hang out in the woods for fun. Not to mention the muddy areas that hadn't dried out and left her sneakers in ruin. No thank you.

Other than the easy clean-up with the handy use of the fire, that is. It was the only aspect of outdoor dining she enjoyed. Okay, so the food was tasty also.

"Let's make sure everything is safely stored from the bears," Connor said, grinning at the kids, "and then we can head out. I'm sure there's a bass or two at the lake with our names on them."

"My name at least," Gabby teased.

"We'll see about that. Beginner's luck this morning," Trey mumbled. It was nice they were finally talking, even if it wasn't like best friends.

"Whatever. We'll know soon enough." Gabby taunted the boy, her confidence in overload mode. Lynette almost wanted her daughter to not catch any more fish just to teach her a lesson in humility. Almost, but not quite.

Trey was having his lack of success heaped on his head. And to an already unhappy kid, it had been like throwing gas on a fire. She'd seen enough of it with middle school kids, both as a teacher and an administrator.

"I'll put Bingo on his leash," Gabby offered as they all prepared to head for the lake.

Connor came to stand next to them. "I've got the poles and tackle boxes. Sorry, Lynette, I only brought three."

The thought of touching bait or a fish was disgusting, their big beady eyes staring at her helplessly. "Fine by me, I don't fish." *Slimy. Scaly. Yuk.*

"She can keep watch for the bears and cougars," Trey said, the boy reminding her of the downside of agreeing to this sojourn into the woods.

"Trey, why don't you lead us down the path? You can do the stick trick to keep us safe," Gabby said as she hooked the lead on Bingo's collar.

"I'm sure we'll be fine, kids. That's enough. Let's not completely scare Lynette off to the great outdoors," Connor said, shaking his head.

Trey stepped off the path. "Sure thing, Dad," he said, picking up two sticks. He started down the trail tapping the sticks together, first on one side of the path and then the other. "I won't say another word."

A silent look passed between Trey and Gabby—the two of them most definitely up to something.

Lynette would have to keep a close eye on them. That is, she would when she wasn't scanning the woods in search of a cougar.. Or any other wildlife that wanted to turn them into an early lunch.

Trey stopped suddenly. "Did you hear that?"

"What?" Lynette asked, peering in the direction he pointed.

Gabby moved to stand next to Trey. "I heard it. It was like a growl or something, right?"

"Trey and Gabby, that's enough," Connor admonished.

Lynette wanted to turn tail and run, but the kids seemed to be taking this in stride.

"Mom, I think you should tap sticks too. We need to make noise they don't like," Gabby said, ignoring Connor's comment.

"Okay," Lynette said, finding it hard to swallow. Or breathe, for that matter. She picked up two sticks and started tapping them together, following Trey's lead.

"I've had enough. This is going too far. Lynette, stop. Tapping sticks isn't going to help. The kids are messing with you." Connor shook his head and smiled as he held out his hand for the sticks.

"But Gabby said she saw it on some show and that it works. What if she's right?" Lynette asked, more than wanting to believe Connor but not ready to give up the only form of defense she had against an attack.

"And I've been camping a long time and have never heard of it before. I knew they were teasing and didn't want to spoil their fun, but this is simply too much." Connor turned to Gabby. "What show did you see it on?" he asked.

Gabby grinned, and Lynette knew she was in trouble. "The Parent Trap. They got their step-mom to do it."

"Yeah, and she looked like a total fool," Trey added, joining in the laughter.

The two of them had set this up at her expense. She felt like a fool, so they'd succeeded. Tossing the sticks to the ground, she started down the trail, not bothering to wait for the others. She was fed up with all of this *and* all of them.

Hopefully, the way to the lake was well marked. *Getting lost would only add to her humiliation.*

It didn't take long after they arrived for Lynette to grow bored. Between the muggy weather, the mosquitoes, and just sitting around watching the others fish, it wasn't her idea of fun. At least the ham and cheese sandwiches and chips they ate for lunch were tasty. Or more importantly, bass wasn't on the menu.

Trey caught two fish back-to-back, and from that point on, there had been an all-out competition between the two kids. At least they were talking, even if only about who was a better fisherman, or fisherwoman, as Gabby liked to call herself. It was a pleasant change from the antagonistic approach they'd all had to suffer through.

This was going to be a long wait for the road to reopen.

Chapter Five

♥

CONNOR APPRECIATED THAT THE kids were getting along better. Earlier this morning on the hike, they'd played a trick on Lynette with the whole cougar thing, but it was harmless to a point. At first, he hadn't nixed their fun, but when he noticed the level of fear on Lynette's face and the way she searched the woods, he felt bad for allowing the teasing to continue.

The fishing at the lake had gone okay, but once the kids had shown signs of boredom, he'd put an end to the activity. It wasn't a hard switch when he mentioned the prospect of swimming. The kids dove right in, while the adults had used a bit more caution. The water had been a little on the frigid side of cool and refreshing. Once back at the campsite, the competition between the kids continued.

Game after game of beanbag toss, boys against the girls, of course. It ended with the girls declared as the winners for the day. A rematch was already planned, Trey unwilling to accept defeat. The surprise ace in the hole on the girl's team turned out to be Gabby. The girl had quite an arm, and her accuracy was spot on—something Connor couldn't fail to appreciate.

Overall, the day had turned out nice. Tonight would be more than a little interesting, given Gabby and Lynette were adamantly against eating the fish he planned for dinner.

While the others had settled in around the campfire, Connor cleaned the catfish and prepared them for a slow roast over the fire. The recipe was simple and used basic ingredients, but it was one his grandfather had taught him. There were lots of fond memories of the times they cooked over a campfire, the two of them camping, fishing, and sharing a love of the great outdoors. A time from before his grandfather's heart attack had robbed Connor of the old man's positive influence.

Lynette added more food and water to Bingo's new bowls. Connor had managed to score not only food but dishes as well, other campers more than willing to lend a hand.

"Do you need any help? With the *ummm*...other food?" Lynette had come up, taking him by surprise.

He grinned. "What? You don't want to cut—" he asked, holding one of the catfish up close to her face.

She jumped back. "No! Not a chance."

Connor decided to press the issue. He really didn't want to waste food and cook it if they truly had no plans on eating it. There was no way to know how long they were stuck here, and food needed to be conserved. "But you will try a bite, right?"

Lynette scrunched up her nose. "Maybe. My decision will come when I see and smell it."

He shook his head. "It's no different than ordering fresh fish at a restaurant. And a hundred times better than ordering fast food fish sandwiches or buying frozen fillets at the grocery store. At least this way, you know where it's coming from and where it's been."

"You have a point," Lynette said.

"Of course, I do. You can peel and cut up the potatoes. Those need to go in a pot of water and be put on the stove at the same time as the fish." Connor pointed to the bag on the picnic table. He enjoyed teasing Lynette and being right. Without trying, she'd turned what was normally considered the boring chore of preparing dinner into fun.

"I'll get right on it." She reached out and touched his arm. "Thanks again for being so good about us staying here, and I'm sorry I was no help setting up the tent. I've never camped, so this is all new to me."

"Don't worry about it. We'll make the best of a bad situation." Although in truth, it wasn't bad at all. In fact, today had been enjoyable. He wasn't sure Lynette would say the same about today's events, which is why he'd gone ahead and made reservations for four kayaks tomorrow. Hopefully, kayaking would be something she'd enjoy.

Connor added the final touches by sprinkling a moderate amount of blackened seasonings on the fillets, squeezing some lemon juice on them, and adding several pats of butter. He sealed the tin foil tightly to keep the liquid and heat in. He did the same with corn, using butter, salt, and pepper for flavor.

With dinner laid out on the grill he'd set up across the flames, the four of them sat around the fire, Bingo more than content to lie at Lynette's feet after an active day. The birds overhead cried out as they started to settle in for the night, while silence was more the norm on site D33. Connor racked his brain for some common ground.

There was always weather, jobs, and school for the kids, to talk about. The weather was unremarkable compared to the recent rainstorms. The next best thing would be the subject of employment. "I know you just moved here, but what kind of work do you do, and are you looking for a job? Maybe I could help."

Lynette shook her head. "Thanks for the offer, but we moved here because I already have a job. I'm a school administrator."

"Really?" They had more in common than he'd first believed. "That makes two of us...at the school, that is." Although Connor working at the school wasn't by choice. He'd much rather be out on a ballfield. "I'm a teacher at Bellevue middle school."

Gabby glanced up at him, a frown on her face. "Mom—"

"Yes, honey, it is. I'm the new principal at Bellevue. What a coincidence."

"The new principal?" Connor hadn't expected this twist.

"You've got to be kidding me," Trey said, his voice full of disgust as he shot Connor an angry glare. "It's bad enough we have girls camping with us, but of all the people, she," he jerked his thumb toward Lynette, "is my principal."

Connor winced. No student would want to be caught camping with the principal. "It would seem that way."

"That means we're all going to be at the same school every day?" Gabby rolled her eyes. "Here I thought it was bad to be saddled with my own mom as principal, but it would seem we are all stuck with each other. And he's," she said, pointing at Trey, "irritating as all get-out."

"Am not, pipsqueak. You're just a know-it-all silly girl." Trey scuffed the ground with his feet, sending some of the gravel toward the fire. "Dad, you do realize this means she's your boss. How weird is this?" It wasn't something Connor had thought of until his son mentioned it.

Lynette frowned and shook her head. It was obvious she was trying to rein in her frustration with the kids bickering. "You two need to stop. It's not helping the situation one bit. And Connor—he's right, you know. It is a little weird."

She didn't know the half of it, at least when it came to the school. The kids, she understood all too well, and she was spot on—they were ramping up the tension all the way around. First chance he got, Connor intended to have a chat with Trey privately about his incessant picking on Gabby. "Weird isn't the best word. Wrong would be closer. People around town have a propensity for talking, but the school board has a propensity for acting. Rumor or otherwise if you get my drift." Connor didn't need the board questioning and challenging every move he made, and all because they wanted to spin his every action as though it were covered in the unseen benefit of the new principal's favor.

"Well, then, we need to make sure word of this little camping escapade doesn't get out," Lynette said, her voice filled with tension.

It would be even more difficult for her, seeing as she had the senior position—not to mention the newest staff addition. "I agree. Kids, no talking about it at school. Deal?" he asked, looking to each of them for confirmation.

"Deal," they said in unison.

"It's not like I'd want anyone to know I spent the weekend with pipsqueak over here and her principal mom," Trey said, his earlier animosity back in full swing.

"Stop calling me that. I'm almost as big as you are," Gabby chimed in. "And the feeling is mutual."

Gabby was tall for her age, not to mention athletically built. Next year, she'd do well to join one of the sport's teams at the school. He easily recognized her natural ability and knew without a doubt she'd be an asset to any team. Connor could even put in a good word for her if she was interested.

The school had tried to force him to do extracurricular coaching or supervision of activities, but he hadn't given in to the pressure. He was only the PE teacher, and that's how it would remain until he got called back to the minor league team.

"I think dinner's almost ready. Why don't we table this discussion and move on to washing up and setting out the plates, napkins, and silverware," Connor asked, ready for a change in subject. Lynette was his boss. It was an unsettling thought because throughout the day, he'd been aware of her as an attractive woman with a pleasant laugh and a soft smile—thoughts he would now need to irradicate.

Lynette sent him a grateful look. "Thanks. Sounds like a great idea." She hadn't said much about the work issue other than to agree. It wouldn't go well for either of them if anyone wrongly suspected that there was something between them. The problem was, in Hallbrook, rumors took off like wildfire, while the truth was slow to follow.

A fact that could put both their jobs in jeopardy unless handled correctly.

Connor opened the tinfoil and placed the catfish in the middle of the picnic table. "Doesn't this look amazing?" he asked, pleased with the way the meal turned out.

"*Ummm*...it looks like fish. A fish I caught." Gabby shot a triumphant glance at Trey.

"All the more reason you need to try it," Connor said, using the opening to convince the girl to try something new.

Gabby nodded. "Fine. Just a little." She held up two fingers less than a half-inch apart. Hardly enough to get a good taste, but that's what he slid onto her plate. Or close enough, adding more to entice her to try a bigger piece.

"Lynette?" He was confident of his success in turning the ladies onto campfire catfish, but they had to try it to make that happen.

"It does look normal. And it doesn't smell like fish, which is a plus," she said, eyeing the catfish. "Just a small taste. Way less than you gave Gabby. I wouldn't want to waste something you so obviously love." Lynette grinned, pushing her plate toward him.

"That's considerate of you, but I assure you, there's plenty." Connor scooped a normal-sized helping onto the doubting Lynette's plate.

He served Trey a generous portion and then placed a big serving on his own plate. "Help yourself to the potatoes and corn."

One by one, everyone loaded their plates with the side dishes. Connor waited in anticipation for the final test...the taste test. He took a bite, making sure it was perfection. "Hmmm, you'll love this, I promise. Soft, sweet fillets, bursting with spice, lemon and butter, and a touch of parsley. Dig in," he said.

Gabby glanced at Lynette, the two exchanging I-dare-you looks.

"Fine," Lynette said, taking the tiniest piece possible. Tentatively, she put the fork in her mouth and chewed, ever so slowly. "Interesting. Not at all what I expected." She went back for another normal-sized piece and ate it. "Actually, this is quite good. I like the spicy kick. Not too much either, just right."

"Told you." He grinned. Connor hadn't met a person yet who didn't enjoy the taste of freshly cooked fish; *if* they ate fish, that is. "Your turn, Gabby," he said, encouraging the girl.

She nodded. "If Mom likes it, I'm sure I will too. It's just getting over the part where I caught it." Gabby's honesty was refreshing and understandable.

"Maybe you're just looking at it the wrong way. God put the fish in the seas to help feed people. It's the reason they're here in the first place," Connor said.

Gabby remained silent for a bit, clearly thinking over his words. Finally, she nodded. "This is still different. It's weird."

"Scaredy Cat. Just eat it, for crying out loud. *Girls,*" Trey said, shaking his head and rolling his eyes in frustration with the whole process.

"Don't be a brat," Gabby quipped, taking a bite to prove she wasn't afraid. "Wow, this is really good, Mr. Weston."

Connor knew the fish would be a hit, and he wasn't above pointing out he was right. "Told you. Eat up; there's plenty more." At least they wouldn't go hungry if they ran out of food. Fish could be fixed lots of ways, and although earlier he joked about having it for breakfast, it was always a possibility.

Chapter Six

❤

LYNETTE WOKE UP COLD and tired, her body sore from sleeping on the hard ground. Granted she had a sleeping bag courtesy of Connor's generosity, but the material did little to soften the impact. She glanced at Gabby, her even breathing a sign she was still sound asleep. Children were obviously far more adaptable to changes than adults.

Bingo was of like mind with Gabby, raising his head to investigate what Lynette was doing, before laying back down. The dog was curled up next to Gabby, and Lynette grabbed her phone and took a picture, wanting to capture the memory. Yesterday's activities had worn them both out.

Wide awake, Lynette had to get up, Mother Nature calling. She changed back into her own shirt and folded the T-shirt Connor had graciously given her to wear. Lynette stepped outside, only to find Connor already up, the fire started, and coffee cooking.

"Good morning," she said, joining him and holding her hands out toward the fire for warmth.

"Morning. Sleep okay?" he asked, his voice husky in the early hours of the day.

"Not especially," she said, shrugging. "Last night reminded me of the *Princess and the Pea* story." And she had lots of time to think about it considering she tossed and turned and was awake through the better part of the night.

Connor handed her a cup of black coffee. "How's that?" he asked, a confused expression on his face.

Of course, he wouldn't know the fairytale—he had a son. "It's a story about a princess seeking shelter from the rain. The prince's mother tests her by secretly placing a pea under a huge stack of mattresses. If the woman had a sleepless night, it would prove she was a real princess. Clearly, I should have been a princess since every little bump on the ground felt like a giant-sized boulder in my back." She laughed, imagining herself wearing a tiara.

Connor smiled. It was a sight she could get used to—and one that was as enjoyable as the hot coffee she was sipping, the flavor and aroma never better. Either that, or she needed caffeine desperately. *Probably the latter.*

"I'll see what I can do to make it better for tonight, my lady," Connor retorted.

"Thank you, kind sir. I'd be much obliged." His light teasing and the dark brew were more than enough to brighten her mood. The man had a certain undeniable charm when he chose to turn it on. And last night was no exception as she recalled the campfire under the stars they shared. "Our kids have great imaginations."

"Storytelling is always fun, especially when camping. My grandfather and I would take turns like we did last night, and the stories we created were some of the best. There were always ghosts and bad guys though, unlike the add-ins from you and Gabby." He chuckled.

Lynette thought the dancing unicorns and puppy dog chaos were sweet twists to the guy's constant efforts to steer the story in a scary direction. "What happened to your grandfather, if you don't mind me asking? It seems you two were close."

Connor nodded, the smile slipping from his face. "He had a heart attack. Completely unexpected, and it was a great loss to our family. He was a hard-working, rock-solid kind of guy you could depend on."

"What about your father?" His honesty prompted the question, and if truth be told, she was interested in learning more about Connor Weston—as a teacher, of course.

"He took off a long time ago. He didn't care much for a son who couldn't make the cut on a little-league team." Connor's voice was filled with bitterness, the sound heartbreaking.

It was a vulnerability she hadn't expected. Lynette struggled to find the right words. "Surely that's not the only reason he left. Sometimes children perceive things differently than they really are."

"I was there; you weren't." Connor shifted in his seat, leaning forward to stir the fire. "Anyway, I hope you like your coffee black as I didn't pack any creamer. I do have milk if you're desperate." The change in topic was obviously his way of bringing an abrupt end to the conversation.

It was better this way. It's not like she wanted to discuss her past either. "Black is fine. Personally, I thought this was tasty. I use flavored creamers at home, Starbucks style, but I think out here roughing it, caffeine is good no matter how it's served."

"Why doesn't that surprise me? I bet back in Boston you drove to a local café for coffee every morning," he teased. Connor's smile was back in place, and the personal introspection moment was over.

"You'd lose." She chuckled.

Woof. Woof. Bingo was awake and ready to join the fun. Lynette let him out of the tent, grabbing his leash off the floor. "I'm going to walk up to the ladies' restroom, and I'll be right back. Can you keep an eye on Bingo since they don't want animals inside the building?"

Connor stood and held out his hand. "Sure, I'll even take him for a quick walk to do his business."

"Thank you, that's sweet of you." Lynette moved to pass him the leash, Bingo pulling and jumping in excitement, eager to say hello. The dog surged forward, knocking Lynette off balance and right into Connor's rock-hard chest.

He reached up to steady her, their gazes locking. "Well, don't let it get around. It'll ruin my image," Connor said, his voice low and gravelly.

It took her a moment to recover from their proximity and the surge of adrenaline rushing through her. She swallowed hard. "My lips are sealed," she said, trying to turn the moment into one of humor.

His gaze drifted to her lips as though he were considering a kiss.

Talking about her lips was the last thing she should have mentioned. "Thanks, I've got to go. Literally." She turned and walked away. Okay, so maybe it was more of a run. Lynette tried to put the way Connor looked at her out of her mind. It wasn't something she could dwell on—the man off-limits considering she is his boss.

The walk to the restroom building wasn't long, but it wasn't something she enjoyed either. Down the hall was more her style—another strike against camping.

By the time she returned to the campsite, Connor and Bingo had settled in by the fire, with still no sign of the kids. "You should have seen the size of the spider in the doorway. He looked poisonous if you ask me. That's what took me so long. I had to try and get around the thing without him dropping or jumping on me. Ugh!" Lynette shivered.

Connor smiled. "There aren't many poisonous spiders in New Hampshire, but we do have some seriously big ones. I'm sure it was just looking for a nice cozy building to spend the night and some warmth from the early morning chill. That makes him not much different than you."

Oddly enough, Connor was right from that aspect, but being compared to a spider was not funny. Okay, so maybe a little funny. "Are you trying to say I have eight legs?" she teased, joining in the fun.

"Maybe not eight, but they are nice," Connor said, shooting a wink in her direction. And just like that, she was reminded of earlier, and that if she hadn't moved, he might have kissed her.

"Well then, *ummm*, thank you, I guess," she stammered, her face flushed warm and most likely beet red. Being a flirt must be part of his job in the minor leagues because it certainly came naturally to Connor. Playing to the adoring fans. To Lynette, it was a long-lost art. "Must be nice to be able to sleep in the way the kids are." She steered the conversation to a safer topic, especially given the direction her own thoughts had taken.

"I agree. Training camp forced me to become an early riser, a habit I've never given up. I've got another full day planned out. Dual-purpose—wear them out and help them learn to get along. It will make our life easier until we can leave." Another good point.

"My motivation to be an early riser was having a kid at home, and then a load of kids at work all day. Mornings are the only time I have peace and quiet." And it was an effort to see more of Dirk, but he was always gone by four-thirty making in next to impossible to have quality time together. Lynette wasn't willing to go that far since it would require a nap at lunchtime—a luxury she couldn't afford.

"I hear you there. I'll start breakfast. I'm sure their growling stomachs will bring them crawling out of the tents long before they are wide awake." Connor stood, stoking the fire a bit.

"As long as it's not a growling bear, I'm okay with that," Lynette said, glancing around just to be sure as a way of reassurance. She couldn't begin to fathom why anyone would voluntarily sleep out here. Not with the chance of bears coming to take your food, or other critters determined to find whatever you mistakenly left out the night before. And then there were the bugs, the flying and crawling kind. With three mosquito bites already, she was maxed out on reasons not to camp.

Connor shook his head and headed for the food pantry, lowering it to the ground. Bingo followed him, ignoring Lynette, knowing all too well where the food was stored. Either that or her dog was a traitor.

"What's for breakfast?" she asked. "Hopefully, you were kidding about the catfish. As good as it was for dinner, I'm not sure I could eat it for breakfast."

"I was teasing. We have plenty of food to last a few days, but if it was a choice between starving and fish for breakfast, I'm sure you would find a way to choke it down."

"Fish omelets. *Hmmm*...yummy. Not." Lynette laughed, grossed out by the image in her head.

"You're in luck. We're fresh out of catfish. Actually, it's a pancake morning." Connor returned to the picnic table with a box of food supplies. Bingo sniffed the air, trying to get a sense of what was available.

"Wow. That sounds delicious. Campfire pancakes." Her stomach agreed just thinking about them. She made her way to the pantry to get the dog's breakfast.

"It's a healthy recipe, so be careful...you might not like it." Connor chuckled.

She emptied the cup of food in the dog's bowl, Bingo practically pushing her out the way to eat. "Good morning to you too, Bingo," Lynette said, patting him on the back.

Moving to Connor's side, she watched as he prepped the batter. "I have nothing against healthy, just not foods I haven't tried and a few other oddities. Why, what's in it?" She almost hated to ask. There was no telling what an athlete of his caliber would consider healthy.

"Cottage cheese and yogurt." To prove his point, he picked up each of the containers, scooping some into the bowl. He continued to dump in the ingredients and mix them around, adding a splash of orange juice.

"You weren't kidding. I can't imagine pancakes with—"

"Trust me."

Lynette frowned, not willing to trust anyone who thought fish for breakfast was a good idea. "You seem to ask me to do that a lot."

"Well, I'm trustworthy." There wasn't an ounce of low self-confidence in the guy. But then perhaps that's what distinguished the difference between an average ballplayer and a successful one. Making it to the majors would be based not only on skill, but also on timing—at least to her way of thinking.

"If last night was anything to go by, I guess you get another pass. Looks like I'll be eating cottage cheese and yogurt for breakfast. What next? Tempeh sausage," she teased. He wasn't the only one with a sense of humor.

Connor glanced up at her in surprise. "That sounds disgusting."

Lynette grinned. "It's nice to know you have limits."

"I do at that." He scooped some batter out of the bowl and formed three small circles in the frying pan, setting it on the grill to let the fire cook the pancakes.

"I have this recipe...I'll have to cook it for you sometime, seeing as you keep cooking for us," Lynette said, deciding turnabout was fair play.

"Please tell me you're joking," he said, his furrowed brow a reward for all his fish jokes.

"I am, but in all honesty, a friend fixed me some once and it was really delicious. It's all in how it's cooked. I'm not even sure where the recipe would be now considering everything I own is in boxes." It had been good, just something she'd never found the time to make for herself and Gabby.

"I'm glad you can't find the recipe. And since you can't, I'll let you return the favor and cook for us when we get back to civilization." His gaze never left her face, the comment not only surprising but intriguing. The man had just invited her to cook for him. *Like a date.*

"Remember, we agreed that's not a good idea—us hanging out together after we get back. I could secretly bake you something as repayment and drop it on your doorstep. You do live next door, or at least you do until I find my own place," she corrected. It was better to keep them both thinking clearly on this issue. It would be all too easy to let her guard down around the man's charming smile and warm, chocolate eyes.

Connor grinned, shooting her a wink. "You're right, boss. A pie or cake would be better. Light of course—I'm watching my weight." He returned his focus to the pancakes, allowing her time to secretly reflect on all she knew about Connor without his all-knowing eyes watching her.

As a father, he was missing some key moments with Trey, but he seemed to care about his son. As a man, he was kind and helpful and had a good sense of humor, but it seemed as though something was holding him back from happiness. As a ballplayer, well, that's the area she knew the least about. Connor had been good enough for the minor leagues once upon a time and had a dream to return...with his sights still set on making it to the majors. Most kids had dreams of making it big in athletics, but Connor was a man now. One with a son who needed him. At his age, she would think he was almost past his prime. Something Connor refused to admit.

And then there was his role as a PE teacher. A role that came under her watch. It was this role she understood the least, not having a chance to see him in action. It was as though he resented the job at times. Come the first of the week, Lynette would make it a priority to rectify the situation and find out more about what he brought to the school and the children entrusted in his care.

He handed her a plate of golden pancakes. "There's maple syrup on the table. Let me know what you think," he said, returning to the fire and pouring out more batter.

She fixed her plate and took a bite, a lot less nervous about the pancakes than she was about the fish. To her surprise, they were yummy. "These are really good. I don't understand how it's possible, but I think I like these more than regular pancakes."

"Told you, you have to trust me."

"I see that. I'm beginning to agree." She smiled, helping herself to more of the delicious pancake.

Connor walked over to one of the tents and pounded his hand on the side. "Wake up, Trey. Time for breakfast if you want it hot. Day's a-wasting." He repeated the same thing with Gabby, the kid's grumblings loud enough to be heard across the campsite.

"Are you sure that was such a good idea? We could have had a quiet meal," she teased.

"True, but then when they got up, I'd still have to cook and clean all over again. No, thank you."

Connor finished cooking the pancakes, a fresh stack at the ready as the kids came out of their tents. Dressed in sweatshirts and sweatpants, their hair a mess, they moved toward the picnic table in search of food. Lynette smiled. To be a carefree kid again—such was life.

"Morning, Gabby and Trey. I already ate the first three pancakes since you weren't out here, so these are fresh off the skillet." She handed them each a plate with two pancakes.

"Why do these look funny?" Gabby asked, her nose scrunched up as she inspected the food offering.

Lynette grinned. Gabby was a lot like her when it came to food. "Cottage cheese and yogurt."

Her daughter frowned, setting the plate back on the table. "Seriously? Do you all not eat any normal food?"

"Sure we do, but this is normal to us. Just because it's healthy doesn't mean it's not better than the original. Ask your mother," Connor said, picking up the plate and holding it out to Gabby.

"If you say so. I'm hungry, so there's not much of a choice." She took the plate from his hand. At least there's maple syrup I can drown it with." Gabby grinned.

"They're good. He's not kidding," Trey said, backing up his dad.

Gabby raised her eyebrows and shot him a look of disbelief but remained silent.

The rest of breakfast went smoothly, and clean-up was in record time. The lure of today's plans a good motivator after Connor announced he'd rented four kayaks online, the facility having reopened after the storms. It was something else she'd never done, but Lynette was more than willing to try.

At least out on the lake, there would be fewer bugs.

Chapter Seven

♥

Connor and Lynette moved to stand next to their kayaks. The kids would hopefully work together and ignite a little team spirit. Bingo ran ahead and played at the water's edge, getting his paws wet. His suggestion to let Bingo ride with him on his kayak was the only reason Lynette had agreed to the adventure, as she didn't want to leave the dog behind in the tent.

"Grab on to the strap at the front. It's the lighter end," he said, walking to the back. They carried the two kayaks closer to the shoreline. Connor's kayak was different, the front end flat and wide open, making it ideal for Bingo to ride safely with him.

After one last trip back to the rental booth, he grabbed four sets of paddles and handed them out to the group, as well as their life jacket. "The rental company makes these mandatory while on the water, so suit up."

"That's lame. I know how to kayak," Trey said while putting it on.

Connor didn't justify the comment with an answer since his son was doing what he was asked. The less confrontation in front of the ladies, the better. Lately, his son, it would seem was quick to gripe about anything Connor told him to do.

"I'll help you two get in the kayak and shove off since you haven't kayaked before. Once out on the water, I'll give you a quick lesson in paddling and then let you play around and figure out what works best for you," Connor offered, trying to be helpful for their first experience.

"That sounds like a good plan," Lynette said, nodding in confirmation.

"I can do it myself," Gabby said, her chin going up a notch. "How hard can it be? Put kayak in the water. Get in. Paddle. A kindergartner could do this."

Someone obviously got up on the wrong side of the bed this morning unless there was something else going on in the girl's head—which wouldn't surprise Connor at all. The changes both she and Trey had been through this past year were certain to influence their behavior. It was why he cut his son some slack, and now, he'd do the same for Gabby. "That's fine. You're welcome to try while I help your mother." Connor pushed one kayak into the water, letting the front half float. He held out a hand for Lynette. "Ready?"

"Sure, thanks." She stepped closer, eyeing the kayak with care. "That's a small area, like kid-size. Are you sure I'm supposed to fit in there? I like yours better. Maybe I should take the dog."

Connor grinned. "You'll fit, trust me. It's not a good idea to have you try to control the dog and learn to kayak at the same time. Put one foot in, hold on to the cockpit sides to steady yourself, and then lower your body as you put the other leg in. I'm right here and will hold the kayak steady." It was a tight fit, but then it was supposed to be. This wasn't boating where you could lounge out and sunbathe or walk around. A kayak was meant to maneuver efficiently and with grace as it skimmed through the water.

"Okay, then. You're the boss, at least for the moment," Lynette teased. Her shoulder-length hair blew in the light breeze as she lowered herself into the cockpit. She shot him a look of gratitude when she was finally in and settled.

He handed her the paddles and pushed her kayak forward until it was completely afloat. Trey was already out in the water, having managed it all on his own. Gabby didn't have the same luck.

"Good job getting settled in the cockpit, Gabby. Next time, if you slide the kayak more into the water before you get in, it will make it easier. You just have to use care balancing yourself in the process. You have two choices from here. Use a paddle to push down and back in the sand to propel you forward, using alternating sides until it breaks free. It will help take the weight off the bottom, and you keep working until you're free from shore and floating." Connor had opted to go the telling route versus asking the girl if she needed help. This way, she had some of the information needed in case she remained on the stubborn side of things.

"What's the second option?" Gabby asked, choosing instead to swallow her pride.

"I can push you forward," Connor said, a teasing grin on his face.

Gabby rolled her eyes. "Fine, just do it."

After pushing Gabby's kayak into the water and giving it a shove, he went back to his own. "Bingo, here boy," he called out.

The dog came running and jumped toward him, fully expecting to play. *Woof. Woof.*

"Down, boy. Come here," he said, patting the spot on the front of his kayak. The dog took a few steps and stopped. "It'll be all right. Trust me," he said, trying to coax the dog onto the boat.

It took a few minutes, Bingo stopping and starting, and way more interested in playing before Connor managed to get him settled. "Stay, boy. Lie down." Bingo did as he was commanded, and soon Connor was afloat and paddling toward the others. They all floated close together, except his son, of course. Heaven forbid if he had to listen to his father give instructions.

"First, make sure the curve of your paddle arcs to the front. There's a button in the middle of the paddle to adjust the angle of the two ends, but I've set you both to zero degrees until you figure out the basics of paddling. Then you can play with what works best. We won't go fast today, that way you can have time to work on correct techniques."

"Good grief. Put the paddle in the water and stroke. Got this, Mr. W.," Gabby said, paddling away. Apparently, one small concession was all she was willing to make.

Lynette paddled closer to him. "Sorry. She's at that age where she knows everything. It's not just you," Lynette said, watching her daughter pull away and head toward Trey.

Connor was all too familiar with know-it-alls. He dealt with them every day at school and at home with his son. "Now that's something we can agree on. Kids this age do think they know everything, and it's our job to figure out the balance that gives them wings. Safely."

Lynette nodded. "Not an easy task."

"No, it's not. Back to technique. It is quite simple with a few basics. If you only put the end of the paddle into the surface of the water, not digging down, you'll use less energy which means the trip will be more enjoyable and last longer."

"Duly noted. I like the sound of that." Lynette tried a few strokes, slowly going through the motions.

The sun beat down on her face, and he noted the intensity of her efforts as she tried to maintain a steady rhythmic pattern of paddling.

Kayaking was relaxing and one of his favorite activities outside of baseball and fishing. It was a time to reflect on life—become one with Mother Nature. Something he needed to do a lot of lately. Exploring the back channels and bays, watching for wildlife and birds, and even dropping in a line. And then there were the handful of occasions he trolled with the kayak and managed to catch a fish. Of course, any time you caught something it was exciting.

With the dog on board, none of that would happen, but it was a small price to pay. At least they were out on the water. He was lucky the rental place had one of the sit-on-top kayaks, but then they weren't as popular as a regular kayak.

Lynette continued to practice the paddle strokes, Connor paying close attention and wanting to make it a pleasurable outing. "Not bad. Next, keep your elbows tucked and your hands loose, as if you're holding an egg. It's really more of a push stroke than a pull stroke."

She tried to twist around to see him. Not an easy task in the life jacket and limited space. She used her paddles to turn the kayak around. "What does that mean?" she asked.

"It means, use the left arm to push the right paddle backward in the water. Versus using the right arm to pull the right side back. Pushing is easier than pulling." Okay, putting it that way, no wonder it was confusing.

"Makes sense." Her answer surprised him.

"Thanks." He'd almost lost himself in the explanation and was grateful he wouldn't have to repeat it.

"Now for the practical application," Lynette said. "You're really good at the teaching thing. I bet you're an excellent PE teacher. You have lots of patience."

Connor couldn't help the rush of satisfaction at her words. Someone thought he was good at something. It was a novelty for sure. "I try, but trust me, it's not always easy with kids."

"Guess I'll have to see you in action before I agree or disagree." She laughed. Lynette paddled away, covering some good distances as she let the kayak glide through each stroke.

"Very good," he said, paddling to keep up with her.

Up ahead, the kids were paddling around near the edge of the shore. "Can we go now?" Trey hollered.

"Sure thing. Just keep it slow until Lynette and Gabby get more used to this," Connor suggested, knowing full well his son would do what he wanted.

"Whatever you say, Dad." Trey took off, putting distance between them. Gabby took off after him, her paddling stroke not super-efficient, but enough that she was putting distance from the adults.

Lynette looked over at him, a worried frown on her face.

"They'll be fine. We're just heading to one of the back bays that leads to a cormorant nesting area. It's amazing," Connor said, trying to put her at ease. Even if Gabby managed to flip the kayak, she had on a life jacket and Trey was right there with her. His son wouldn't let anything happen to the girl, no matter how tough he tried to act.

"So you're a naturalist and a birder. This is a totally unexpected side of you. I'm impressed," Lynette teased.

"There's probably a lot about me you don't know or wouldn't understand."

"And given the circumstances, should probably stay that way. Don't you think?" Her rebuke was the shove he needed to keep himself in check.

"I agree." Connor hung back, keeping an eye on Lynette and letting her progress at her own speed as she followed the kids. Keeping close to the shore, they made their way to the bay. Thick grasses and tall trees lined the sides, with a few fallen trees poking their branches and limbs through the surface of the water, forcing them to maneuver around.

Lynette suddenly screamed. She started to paddle wildly, splashing water all around.

Adrenaline rushed through Connor, his heart pounding as he began to close the distance between them. "What's wrong?"

Bingo sat up and started to bark, looking as though he wanted to jump in the water and swim to Lynette.

"Bingo, no," he commanded, trying to settle the dog down and steady the boat.

"A snake fell out of the tree and landed on my kayak," she said, the words tight with fear.

Connor double-timed his strokes. "Is he still on the kayak?" At the rate she was going, all the turning, twisting, and thrashing could very well upend the kayak, and dump her into the water in the process.

"No, he slipped into the water, and I can't see him," she cried out, her voice rife with tension.

The kids had started back in their direction. "What's wrong, Mom?" Gabby yelled.

"A snake dropped from a tree and landed on my boat. I don't want to do this anymore. I'm going back." Lynette's face had gone pale, and he was worried about her.

"Those are just water snakes. They aren't poisonous, and he doesn't want to hurt you," Trey called over to Lynette as he neared.

"He's right. That snake would have been more afraid of you than you were of it," Connor said, trying to add reassurance.

"Are. Still am. And you don't know what I felt. I'm going back." Lynette shook her head, still glancing all around, as though positive the snake was going to come back out of the water.

"So we all get our kayak trip ruined because you're afraid of a snake?" Gabby asked, a scowl on her face.

Connor tried to think of a good solution. It was hard work keeping everyone happy, but the trip had been his idea. So much for fun. "Why don't you two go on to the end of the bay, Trey? Just to the nesting area and then back. I'll escort Lynette back to the beach area where we put in and wait for you. With Bingo riled up, it'll be better if I get him back to shore."

Trey nodded. "Works for me." His son puffed up with pride. Being put in charge seemed important to him, even if it was only for a girl.

"And me," Gabby chimed in. "I want to see the nesting area."

"Just don't fall behind, pipsqueak," Trey said, grinning. The kid had a sense of humor.

Gabby shook her head and started to paddle away. "Catch me, slowpoke." But then, so did Gabby.

Trey had met his match. The two took off, neck and neck, cutting through the water, leaving the parents behind without so much as a second glance. "Let's go," he said, turning his focus back on Lynette. The sooner he got her and Bingo back to shore, the better.

"Are you sure they'll be okay?" Lynette asked, a worried expression on her face as she watched the pair put more distance between them.

"I'm sure." Connor and Lynette turned around and headed back. She was looking like a skittish kitten waiting for a dog to pounce. Which is exactly what Bingo would do when they got on shore, the dog having sensed her distress. "We could talk on the way back. It might help."

"Thank you. I'm sorry to ruin the kayak trip. I'm terrified of snakes in case you haven't figured that out."

"I gathered that much. They do exist, but it's not often one sees them." Typically, he only saw a handful each year, something he didn't think would be helpful to share with Lynette.

"The city isn't a place one runs into snakes, or on the air bases where we lived for that matter. I'm glad you're being so understanding and not acting like a macho man talking down to me. Thanks, Connor. You really are a nice guy."

Connor wasn't good enough at a lot of things, but it would seem Lynette thought differently. She made him feel important, strong, and protective. Like he had his life together, and he was enough. Something his father and ex-wife never made him feel. "It's all good, but really, it's nothing. It's what anyone would do to help."

"Not Dirk. My husband put his work first, and the rest of us were expected to be his support team, not the other way around. We lived like that the entire time he served in the military."

"I'm sorry." Connor hated he'd said anything that would make her think of the past. Following her husband around couldn't have been easy, especially raising a daughter on her own by the sounds of things. It made him think of his ex-wife.

Isn't that exactly what he'd done to her? Left her alone to raise Trey. Clearly, he was at fault things didn't work out. But then, her lack of support and faith in him was exactly why he'd pushed himself harder and stayed away longer, to do anything he could to make her happy.

They were both to blame, and perhaps therein lay the reason the marriage failed—they were never in love with each other. Or, at least, not the way they should have been for marriage and trying to build a life together.

The forever kind.

Chapter Eight

♥

FOR FOUR DAYS AND nights, Lynette put up with bugs, fish, snakes, animals, and a hard bed at night. None of which allowed her to get any good sleep. It was a relief when the road reopened, and they were finally able to leave late Monday afternoon.

Trey and Gabby got along tolerably well, given the circumstances. And even she and Connor managed to find some mutual territory by taking turns cooking, cleaning, and even losing at beanbag toss.

The school board understood why she missed the first day she was expected to report to the office. Unfortunately, it also meant they knew she was with Connor, seeing as he was forced to call out of school yesterday as well. This morning, amidst lots of grumbling, she'd finally managed to get

Gabby out the door. After dropping her off at her new homeroom and introducing themselves to the teacher, Lynette made her way to the administration offices.

The receptionist looked up when Lynette entered the office. "Good morning," the woman said. Not a hair out of place, the blonde was the picture of efficiency.

"Good morning. I'm Lynette Taylor." She leaned forward, holding out her hand for a more formal introduction.

"Ah, yes. We've been expecting you. I'm Mary Ellen Walters." The women clasp her hand in a light handshake. "I can't believe you got caught up in the madness when the dam broke and ended up trapped at the state park. Not quite the welcome to Hallbrook you were expecting, I'm sure." Mary Ellen grinned, eyeing her with curiosity.

Lynette had no plans to expand on the information pool. "No, not at all. But I'm here now," she added, preferring to stick to the professional side of things. "I might as well jump right in. If you show me where I belong, I can start by getting familiar with my office, and then if you, or someone else, could show me around the school, that would be great." It was the most effective way to send a direct message that the conversation was over and it was on to business.

Mary Ellen's grin faded. "I'll personally take you on tour. How about in fifteen minutes?" she asked, glancing at her watch.

Mission accomplished. "That sounds great."

"Your office is right through there." Mary Ellen pointed to the door marked principal right behind her desk. The woman stood and led the way, opened the door, and flipped on the light. "Again, welcome to Bellevue Middle School and to Hallbrook. I'm sure you'll love it here."

"Thank you. I'll see you in a bit for the tour."

The phone in the outer office rang. "Got to run." Mary Ellen scurried away, ready to tackle the next issue that popped up. One of many every day that would occur, based on Lynette's past experiences. There were a lot of great kids eager to learn, but where they existed, so too did the ones who found it a boring waste of time and managed to find them-selves in trouble.

Lynette sat behind the desk, testing out the new chair. Glancing around the office, she noted it was rather large. The picture window looked out over the playground, giving her a bird's eye view of all that happened outside. Children raced around, chasing each other. A game of dodge ball off to one side was being played. And then there were the acrobats and daredevils on the swing set. A peaceful, sunny day in school paradise—or so that's the way she liked to think of it.

The job had many challenges, but Lynette loved the kids. Even the ones who acted out. Most children just wanted attention, and it was her job to make sure they got the positive influence they needed to succeed. It was her chance to make a difference.

She got up and walked around, taking inventory of the books and pictures left behind when the last principal quit suddenly and moved away. A sick daughter or something of that nature, judging by the comments made when she'd interviewed for the job. The woman had to give everything up to go watch her grandchildren, but it was a decision Lynette would make all day long. She would do anything for Gabby, now or after she'd left home and started her own family.

"Ready to go?" Mary Ellen asked, appearing in the doorway.

"Sure." Lynette was surprised fifteen minutes had already passed. Other than taking an inventory of her office and watching the children play, she'd accomplished nothing.

"I put the phones on hold so the call will roll to voicemail automatically. Only the teachers can bypass the system, so I'm all yours for the next thirty minutes." Mary Ellen smiled and pointed to the door.

They started down the hall, Mary Ellen pointing out various halls and classrooms, while Lynette tried her best to register the details. The cafeteria was mostly quiet, with only workers cleaning the tables and arranging the chairs for when the mad rush began.

"This is where the band meets," she said, stopping in front of one of the rooms.

Lynette peeked inside, not wanting to disturb the clarinet lessons. The room was set up with a semi arc made up of two rows and chairs, the children's instruments making squeaks and squawks as they tried to play through the *"Three Blind Mice"* song.

The next stop took them outside.

"Over there are the soccer fields." Mary Ellen pointed to the right. "That direction leads to the football field, and the baseball fields are back to the left. Basketball is always in the gym with the indoor courts. Does your daughter play any sports? We have lots of girl's teams for her to choose from."

"Gabby's into baseball. She played little league and was named one of the all-star pitchers."

"Baseball, huh? We have a girls' softball team, and the boys play baseball."

"Are there any rules that say she can't try out for the baseball team?" Lynette asked, all too familiar with the uphill battle they'd faced at a few of the schools Gabby had attended.

"She'd be up against the boys, and we've not had that happen before, but I don't see why not." Mary Ellen shrugged.

"That's what she did in Massachusetts. She's a tough competitor even against the boys." Lynette was proud of her daughter's fierce determination.

This past year she'd thrown herself into practicing harder than ever, most likely to fill the void of her father's passing.

"That's awesome. Tryouts ended in March for this season, but you could talk to some of the teachers who have stepped in to coach the team after our last one took another job in Scranton. Maybe they'd let her at least practice with the team. I'm not sure how all that works honestly, but with everything up in the air, who knows. We've had trouble just getting some of the teachers to volunteer to help out for the rest of the year."

Lynette frowned. The school had a professional level baseball player, and yet by the sounds of things, he hadn't stepped up. "What about the PE teacher? I thought Connor mentioned that he played baseball or something like that?" Lynette added, trying to cover her tracks and not look as though she were an authority on the man's life.

"Oh, yeah, he played. Still would if he had his way. Connor was in the minor leagues, but an injury, or fate, got in the way of his dream to be called up to the majors. He quit to take care of his son, but still wants another shot at the pros. It's why he refuses to help—keeping himself free for the call or some such nonsense. It's too bad because he'd be perfect for the coaching position."

"Such a shame not to use a God-given talent to help the kids," Lynette said, voicing her opinion as an administrator. On a personal level, she couldn't imagine him *not* helping, and it was disappointing to find out it was intentional. Not that he hadn't been asked.

Mary Ellen nodded. "He's a great guy, but he has one eye on the exit door if you know what I mean." They reentered the building and continued down the hall for the tour of the building.

"Based on what you said, I get it. The guy doesn't want any serious commitments that he'd have to break if he makes it back to the minors. In a way, I can respect that, but still, I feel awful that the kids are the ones losing out in this situation. I'll have to see what we can do to corral someone, for Gabby's sake. She'd be devastated if she can't play out the rest of this year or all summer, and would be tough to live with." Lynette tried to stay even keel on her answer, not looking to make enemies by taking sides.

"My nephew's the same way. These kids get the ball bug, and there's no stopping the fever." Mary Ellen laughed.

"Gabby's been playing since she was five. I can totally relate," Lynette said.

Mary Ellen's phone rang. The woman frowned as she glanced down at the screen. "Five minutes of peace and quiet left, but it appears to have come to an abrupt halt. Oh, well. Duty calls." She pressed a button to accept the call.

"This is Mary Ellen," she answered. "I see. Who is it?" she shook her head. "Oh. Not good. His father won't be a happy camper. We're on our way back to the office now." Mary Ellen hung up and slid the phone into her pocket.

Judging by the comments, Lynette was about to jump in feet first on the job. "What's wrong?" she asked.

Mary Ellen frowned. "One of our boys got caught cheating on a test. The math teacher, Mr. Lawson, is escorting the student to the office. We need to head back there to meet up with them." The woman had only hesitated slightly but it was long enough to make Lynette wonder what she wasn't telling her.

"Is this a regular problem child?" Lynette asked, trying to prepare herself for the part of the principal role she liked least. *Discipline.*

Again with the hesitation. "Not normally. This school year has been rough on the kid. His parents are divorced. You know the drill when that happens," Mary Ellen said.

"I do." It didn't mean Lynette had to like it. "So who's the kid?" she asked.

"That's the other part of the problem," Mary Ellen said, stopping in her tracks and turning to face Lynette. "It's a teacher's son, and there's a more delicate balance to be maintained. I'm sure you know about the dangers of anyone seeing favoritism or going easy on a kid because of the parent connection. No matter what the home status is, we have to be tough on the child or face other parents' wrath."

Lynette knew all too well the dangers and the balancing act. Teachers' kids were always the hardest to know the right amount of discipline. "That's so true. I'll think of something after I talk to the student. What's his name?" she asked as they resumed a brisk pace back to the office.

"Trey Weston. Connor Weston's kid."

She stopped, grabbing the woman's arm. "Trey? Oh, no. This isn't good."

"How do you...oh, that's right. You were camping with them when the dam broke." The woman looked at her, a question in her eyes.

Lynette had to set the record straight. "No, not camping with them. Picking up Gabby. There's a huge difference. I didn't want my daughter hanging out with a man I'd never met, regardless of the circumstances." She didn't care if she was casting doubt against Connor. It was more important for this woman not to assume what happened had been a voluntary event.

"I see. But you still ended up camping together, so you should be well-versed in Trey's recent attitude issues. And his father's reluctance to commit to Bellevue one hundred percent. Always one foot out the door." Mary Ellen nodded, doing some introspection of her own and clearly coming to her own conclusions.

"I don't think it's appropriate to discuss their personal affairs. Let's stick with Trey and his school issues," Lynette said, firmly establishing her authority and her limits.

"Okay, then. Now's your chance."

They rounded the corner and came face to face with Mr. Lawson and Trey. The man looked like a math teacher, his large spectacles and thinning hair making him appear quite studious and meek. *More like an accountant.*

"This is Brian Lawson, our math teacher. And that's Trey, as you already know," she said, pointing to the kid sitting on the bench outside her office. "Brian, meet the new principal, Lynette Taylor," Mary Ellen said, making the introductions.

"Sorry it's under these conditions, but it's nice to meet you." Brian shook her hand, his grip surprisingly strong. Nothing meek about the man. "He was texting answers to a couple of kids in class. It's not the first time this has happened. Trey's smart as a whip, but unfortunately, makes some dumb decisions. I really had no choice but to turn him in."

The man looked apologetic, and he shouldn't. This was about teaching children, and part of that was a correction to help them make better choices. "It's nice to meet you also, and I understand your concerns, but bringing this to our attention is the right thing to do. But I do have one question—where are the others?" Lynette asked.

Brian frowned. "Others?"

Part of her wanted to say *do the math*, but she resisted, sticking to professionalism. "The kids that Trey texted the answers to. Surely they are just as complicit in all this."

Brian's face flushed red as he pulled at his collar. "I just thought we should start with the source. Not involve the other parents yet, especially if we don't have to."

This was discrimination in reverse, and Lynette didn't like it. "I see. You feel we should take the easy route and discipline Trey because he's a teacher's son and let the other two kids get a pass. I think all three made bad decisions, and all three should have consequences. Please give the names to Mary Ellen, and I'll expect the other two in my office shortly. Mary Ellen, please notify the student's parents and set them up with an appointment to meet up with me. Thank you," Lynette said, keeping her voice level and professional.

Brian didn't look pleased, but he had enough good sense to keep his mouth shut.

"Sure thing," Mary Ellen said, nodding as she stepped around her desk.

Lynnette didn't miss Trey's look of surprise even though it disappeared quickly, as he aimed for the cool, uncaring posture and attitude.

"Trey, in my office. Now," she added when he didn't move.

His surly expression deepened, but without a word, he stood, turned, and walked into the office.

Lynette paused at the door. "Hold any calls, will you?"

"Sure thing. Good luck," Mary Ellen said, shooting her a wink.

"Firm guidance requires no luck, but thanks." Lynette wanted equality and fair treatment for all the kids, the teachers, and the parents. Hopefully, word would get around fast that she wouldn't tolerate any antics that went against policy.

Lynette moved into the office. "So, what's going on, Trey? You can have a seat, you know. You're not going anywhere until we get to the bottom of this."

The boy scowled at her, not budging from where he stood. "You're not my mother."

Lynette sat down, leaning back in her chair. She didn't want this to be an adversarial meeting, and she did her best to project concern. Children had to believe you cared. "You're right, I'm not. But I am the school principal and therefore in charge of what happens in school and on school property. Guidelines would recommend suspension, so unless that's what you are looking for, you might want to consider sitting down and talking with me."

"I don't care." The expression on Trey's face said otherwise. His tough-guy act was cracking.

"You will. Your father is being notified and I'm expecting him to show up in short order. We all need to talk this out. You're a good kid, Trey. I've seen you in action when you're not trying to act all tough." It was the closest she would come to reminding Trey of the past few days they had camped together. He'd hated the idea she was the principal, but those four days had given her more insight with regards to what made him tick.

Trey shrugged. "What you see is what you get." He sat down, a step in the right direction. Slouched, but sitting.

She had to reach him, get him to discuss what was going on in his head. She had a fairly good idea, and that's where she'd start. "I disagree. Talk to me about your mom. I sense you're angry at her leaving, but you know, it's not your fault. Don't let your parent's decisions mess up your life by causing you to act out. That's letting you mess up your own life. It's a choice."

"What are you, a shrink or something?" Trey glared at her, but at least he was listening.

Lynette shook her head. "No. I've seen this with a lot of kids. I want to help you, trust me."

"Why?" he asked. One word that held a wealth of meaning.

She'd have to tread carefully if she didn't want him to shut down again. "Because I care about you," Lynette said, meaning every word.

"It's your job." He was right, but it wasn't *just* her job.

"It's more than that. I became a principal to help kids reach their full potential. There's more to you than this—I just know it. Your mother leaving isn't your fault," Lynette said, pushing a little harder, confident this was the issue.

Trey scowled. "Sure seems that way."

"Why do you say that?"

"Because she left, and she doesn't care about seeing me or nothing. And Dad, he had to give up his dream to stay home with me. Hardly seems fair. And I know he resents me because of it."

Wow. That was a lot of guilt for a child to handle. Lynette's heart was breaking for the boy. "I can't answer you about your mom as I don't know her. Sometimes people make tough choices, and we don't ever fully understand them. As to your dad, he can take care of himself and make his own decisions based on the cards life deals him. Did you ever think maybe he wanted to quit the minors and be a part of your life? I don't think he resents you, but I do think you should talk to him about it."

Trey didn't say anything, as though considering her words.

"Don't let this current bump in the road destroy your chances of getting into a good college. And what about baseball? You do realize if I suspend you, I will have to take you off the team," Lynette said, pressing forward while she had his attention.

His expression darkened as her words sank in. "Why? That hardly seems fair."

Lynette shrugged. "What's not fair is how hard some of the other kids must study to get their good grades while you were handing out answers to others. I understand you're a math whiz, so why not put it to good use and tutor some of the other kids?" The idea had suddenly occurred to her, and she knew it was the perfect disciplinary action. *Let the punishment fit the crime.*

"Lame. I'd be laughed out of school," Trey said, shaking his head. "No way."

"It's either that, or suspension and no baseball. It's your choice. You've put me in a difficult position, and I'm trying to help you, whether you believe it or not." The alternate-choice method usually worked and Lynette prayed it wouldn't backfire on her this time.

Trey stood and started toward the window, gazing out. "If you suspend the others, everyone will hate me."

Lynette understood where he was coming from. "I'll offer them deals as well. It will be up to them how they decide," she said, trying to reassure him but unable to promise the outcome.

"How long do I have to decide?" he asked.

"Until your dad walks through that door." As if her words conjured up the person, the door opened, and Connor walked in. "Time's up, Trey."

The kid spun around and spotted his father. "Fine. I'll tutor. Two days, during recess."

Lynette said a quick prayer of thanks that he'd come to the right decision. Now all that remained was setting the terms. "One week, during recess, and it's a deal," Lynette offered, confident this would end well.

Trey nodded. "Deal."

Connor stood at her desk, looking back and forth between her and Trey. "So, what's a deal? And what's going on? Mary Ellen said you got in trouble again, Trey. Why do you keep doing this to me?" Connor stood there, jaw clenched, as he waited for answers.

"Chill. It's no big deal." Trey shrugged. Not the best tact to take with his dad.

"It is a—"

Lynette held up her hand to stop Conner. "Trey, why don't you head back to class?" Better to cut him off before he said something he'd regret, or worse, have Trey changing his mind. "Remember, we have a deal. I'll work on the details and let you know."

Trey stood, crossing the room with long strides, eager to get out of the office.

Connor looked dumbfounded as the door closed behind his son. "Why did I come all the way down here just to watch Trey walk out of the office?"

"Because I want to talk to you, Connor. One on one."

He sat down. "What's going on? It's your first day on the job, and I'm called in to see you. I would have thought you had enough of me over the weekend." His attempt at humor to ease the tension in the room was appreciated.

"Enough of camping, not you. Well, maybe that, too. I mean, not like it sounds," Lynette said, stumbling over her words like a schoolgirl.

Connor raised one eyebrow in disbelief. "I'm sure it's exactly like it sounds. But I'm also sure I'm not here to gloss over the merits or demerits of our camping trip."

"No, you're not." It was time to dig in and work on the parenting side of the problem. She hoped he'd listen. "This is about Trey. I know I said a few things the past couple of days to you about your son, and now, more than ever, I'm convinced I'm right. Trey was caught cheating on his math test. It's a classic cry for attention."

Connor shook his head. "Math? It's his best subject. Why would he need to cheat? The teacher must be mistaken."

He was instantly on guard and protective of his son. It was a natural reaction she liked to see as it showed how much he cared, but in this case, it was misplaced protection. "Trey admitted to his part in the cheating. He was the one providing the answers, not receiving them," Lynette adding, clarifying the situation.

"Of all the—"

"Don't say it. He and I worked out a math-tutoring deal, so I'm moving past this incident as far as he's concerned. I'm more worried about the next time if something doesn't change for him."

Lynette took the plunge and dove into the crux of the matter.

"Next time? And what of the other kids? Or is it just Trey in trouble?"

"Who do you think Trey will be tutoring?" Lynette grinned. "That is if they agree to it as an alternative to suspension. I'm sure I can fill the tutoring spots if they choose not to take that route."

"I see. Highly creative, I must say." Connor nodded. "But then why does there have to be a next time?"

This was the tough part, but it was important Connor understand the truth. "There will always be a next time unless you stop the cycle."

"Me? How do you propose I do that? I'm not a magician." Connor leaned back in the chair and ran a hand through his hair.

"No, but you're his father. He wants your attention, Connor. Needs it. His mother left him, and he doesn't understand. He thinks you resent having to quit the minors and raise him. More than ever, he needs you to spend time with him to understand that's not true." She could tell her comment hit hard as the corded muscles of his neck went tight with tension.

Connor let out a deep breath. "And how do you propose I do that? I can talk to him, but with work, and school, and training, not to mention, his practices and games, I'm flat out of time."

In the back of her mind, this is where she'd wanted the conversation to go. "I'm glad you asked."

"You are?" Connor asked, frowning.

Lynette nodded. "I am. What if you coached the baseball team instead of making all the teachers fill in round-robin style until we find a new coach? You're perfect for the position."

"No." His flat rejection stunned her. She'd expected him to think it over at least.

She wasn't giving up this easy. "Why not?"

"I've got too much to do. What happens when I make the minors again and have to split? What happens to the kids then? I'm not a quitter, and I don't want to build up their hopes, only to dash them again."

This was a side of the argument she hadn't considered, but if anything, it only made her more certain he was the right person to coach the team.

At least in the interim. It was trying to find a way to get him to agree that was the problem. "So you admit you care about the kids?"

"Well, yes. Of course. All of them are also my students."

"Then care enough to make this work until your next big shot happens. We'll deal with the fallout on this end when it does. I have confidence you will get whatever you want out of life. So, give the kids a chance to learn with the best. Someone who knows more than most and can give the kids a much greater insight that will benefit them all, even if only for a short time. Your son the most. He needs you to be there for him. It's a win-win situation. Show him you care and that you want to help him. Show him he's the most important thing in your life—not trophies, or titles, or stats. *Him*."

Connor's mouth hung open. Whether speechless or shocked, she wasn't sure. Open. Close. Open. Close. He shifted in his seat and rubbed the back of his neck. "Fine. You have yourself a coach. But only until I have to leave. Understood?"

"Loud and clear. And Connor, it's the right choice whether you want to believe it or not."

"Time will tell. Let's hope you're right." Connor stood and walked out of her office, just as Mary Ellen buzzed her.

"I've got Ethan Samuels and Kenny Stiles here to see you. I've contacted their parents, and their moms are on their way."

"Thank you. Send them in." Hopefully, the other meetings turned out as well as the first two.

"Will do. And boss, I don't know what you said to Connor, but he's one unhappy camper."

"That only makes it fair, as I was an unhappy camper all weekend." Lynette disconnected the speaker, trying to prepare herself for the next couple of rounds with kids and parents.

This would be a long first day.

Chapter Nine

♥

CONNOR STILL COULDN'T BELIEVE he let Lynette goad him into coaching the middle school baseball team. He'd been truthful about how busy he was and could be in the future. It's not as if he hadn't warned her, or even the others every time they'd tried to press him into taking the position since the previous coach left.

But for the duration of his time in Hallbrook, he'd do his part. It was hard to say no to Lynette, but the greater issue was in the fact she'd been right. It would be good for Trey, and as a father who hadn't been around much, it would be best if he helped while he could. And if it helped the other kids and the school at the same time, all the better.

Trey hadn't like being lectured about the stupidity of cheating. The news his father was going to be the new coach of the team had been met with an equal lack of enthusiasm, which was more proof Lynette was on to something. What kid didn't want their father to coach them?

After reminding Trey of what led to all this, he settled down a bit. Connor made sure to point out the alternative and that he should be grateful Principal Taylor hadn't taken him off the team.

Creative discipline was in short supply within the school system—not so with Lynette. Connor appreciated her efforts, and not just for Trey's sake. She would be an excellent school administrator—someone who wouldn't take the easy way out and simply suspend students.

Giving himself time to prepare, he'd pushed practice to the weekend, wanting a couple of extra hours with the team to put forth his plan of action. "We need to get going," Connor said as Trey walked into the living room. "I've got to get to the ballfield early to set up, and we need to have a team meeting to go over the changes and my expectations moving forward."

"I'm ready. It'll give me more time to hang with the guys." Trey picked up his duffel bag of gear and headed for the door.

"And check out the girls watching from the bleachers. I know the routine." Connor grinned, remembering what it was like to be a kid.

"Hardly. It's bad enough I have to put up with them in school, giggling by the lockers as the football guys go by." It sounded like Trey was more than a little jealous of the attention the football team garnered, but then, in middle school and high school, football was king.

"You won't think that in a few years." He tossed the bag of team supplies into the back of the truck and headed for the school.

Pulling into the parking lot, Connor shut off the engine and slid out of the truck. He slung the two duffel bags over his shoulders, Trey doing the same with his own bag. The two of them made their way to the ball field, noting several players were already there.

His son moved off to hang out with a few friends, while Connor talked to parents and kids as they arrived. Right at noon, Connor blew his whistle, calling in the team to start practice. The kids all gathered around, jostling each other and vying for who could get the closest.

"Good afternoon, everyone. In case you haven't heard, I'm the new temporary coach for the ball club. All of you are in my PE class, and I have a good idea of your athletic abilities already. We are going to shake things up with practices, especially starting out, so I can get a feel for what each one of you contributes to the ball team. So consider this a starting over of sorts—a new set of tryouts."

Several kids grumbled and groaned, the starting players feeling the pressure of losing their star role.

"I want everyone to divide up into two teams, A and B, starting down the line with an A player and alternating to the end," Connor instructed, also noting their ability to follow instructions. More grumbling, but at least the players did what they were told.

"Hang on," a woman called out from behind him. Probably a parent already disgruntled with the way he was doing things—something he'd nix right away.

He turned, only to find Lynette and Gabby running his way. The question was, why?

"Can I play with the team, Coach?" Gabby asked in a rush as she drew near.

The request was highly unusual given that tryouts ended in March and the team was already set. Gabby scored points, however, simply by properly addressing him, enough that he paused to consider his answer.

"The team is already set, and I'm not sure I can allow that. I'd have to check the rules, but perhaps you could talk to the softball coach," Connor said, hating the look of disappointment on Gabby's face. A look that was quickly replaced by determination, judging by the firm set of her jaw and stance.

"I don't play softball; I play baseball. All-star with the Boston Mighty Mites little league last year," Gabby said. There weren't many girls who played baseball, and he was more than a little stunned to hear she was named an all-star player. It certainly added a new twist to the situation.

"It's true," Lynette said. "And I checked the rules, just in case. Since she just moved here, the rules allow for a tryout of sorts to see if a player is at a high enough level to be considered as a walk-on to the team. Boy or girl," Lynette added. She'd done her own research and had come prepared to fight for her daughter's right to play with the team.

There were always parents who believed their kid was the best and who didn't understand that not all kids were created equal in athletics. At this level of play, all players who made the team played, but it was also the point where the better players started to rise to the top and played more. *All-star*.

He was holding new tryouts within the team, and it couldn't hurt to give Gabby a chance to prove herself with the others. It was much easier to let her try and fail than to say no, given the circumstances.

"Fine. But only because the team has an open roster spot as one of the kids moved away. What position do you play?"

Gabby grinned. "Pitcher."

Of course. Not only was the empty spot that of the back-up pitcher, but it would be the hardest position for Gabby to compete at. This wouldn't end well, of that, Connor was sure. He hadn't planned to cut any players, but Gabby would be the exception. It's not like she was on the team to begin with.

An image of her throwing beanbags with a high degree of accuracy popped into his head, reminding Connor of the girl's athletic talents.

"Okay, fine. We are down a back-up pitcher, so I'm willing to give you a shot. But no promises. Understood?" Explaining it to the team would be another hurdle he'd have to cross, but he was the coach, and the decision was within his power.

"Understood, Coach."

"Join the others, and I'll introduce you."

Gabby jogged over to the team, not at all timid at the idea of competing with the boys.

"Thanks, Connor," Lynette said, shooting him a broad smile. "You'll be surprised, trust me. I still can't believe how well she plays myself, and I'm her mother. Do you need any help since I, um, sort of forced you into this coaching gig?"

"Sort of?" He quirked one eyebrow up in disbelief. "There's no sort of about the way you wrangled my services. Temporarily, anyway."

"Yes, temporarily. It would seem you're not going to let me forget that little fact, but the offer still stands."

"If you want to help, knock yourself out. I presume you know something about baseball since Gabby plays." It would be good to have someone as an assistant and allow him more time to assess the players, focusing on what was important and not corralling kids at every turn.

Lynette nodded. "I know enough to help. Just tell me what you want me to do."

"Well, since you're dressed for it, why don't you take team B and start running the bases and warm them up. Some calisthenics along the way would be great. But first, let me explain what's going on and introduce Gabby to the team." Judging by the increasingly loud voices drifting his way, the boys weren't happy.

"Can do, although I didn't come prepared to run. These are walking shoes," Lynette said, glancing down at her feet.

Great. An assistant who was more concerned about a fashion statement than working with the team. "If you don't want to do it..."

"I didn't say that. Next time, I'll wear better shoes."

"Next time?" he asked. If Gabby didn't make the team, there would be no next time.

"If you want me, that is," she said, a soft blush tinging her cheeks.

"Of course I want you. As an assistant, that is. It's only right considering it's your fault I'm doing this in the first place. Is this offer made regardless of whether Gabby makes the team or not? I won't give preferential treatment to anyone," he said, making his point clear. Something Lynette should appreciate, given her attitude toward the kids and equality.

"Look, you're coaching for Trey. You keep your eye on the ball and the end game with your son and let me handle Gabby and my offer to help."

"I reckon you know more than you let on," Connor said, her comment referencing the big picture using baseball euphemisms spot on. He turned and walked back to the kids, holding up his hand, showing he wanted silence.

"What's going on, Coach? Why is she here?" Bradley asked, jerking his hand toward Gabby.

"Yeah, why, Coach?" several of the others mumbled. Trey remained silent, a stony expression on his face.

"Good question. The truth is, according to the rules, Gabby Taylor has the right to be accepted on the team as a walk-on since she just moved here. That is, if she can hold her own and prove she deserves to be on the team, that is. This basically means she needs to perform at a level that reflects she would have been placed on the team during the regular season tryouts."

"Girls don't belong on a baseball team," Trey said, sporting a frown as he stepped forward to be heard. The grumblings rose to a loud chatter.

"According to the rules, there is nothing to stop girls from joining the team. They simply must compete at the same level as the boys. I've made no promises, so let's all settle down and get this practice started," he said, addressing the group and taking control. "Remember, you are all trying out to show me what you've got and to help me decide your playing time. The more you give, the more you play. And that includes leadership and attitude abilities. Gabby join the A-team," he said, pointing to the group of boys on the left. He turned to Lynette and indicated for her to stand next to him. "This is Principal Taylor, for those of you who don't know her yet. She's going to be helping us out. Team A fall in behind me. Team B fall in behind Principal Taylor. Let's go—lap time."

Slow at first, the kids picked up speed by the time they rounded second base. He'd picked the A-team since Trey and Gabby were on it—making it easier to keep an eye on both.

Connor pulled up alongside Trey, keeping pace with him. "Everything okay?" he asked, using the opportunity to have a private conversation with his son.

"Hardly. The guys aren't thrilled with your re-tryouts and even less thrilled with Gabby being here. Why would you let her try out? Wasn't last weekend more than enough time with the Taylors?" Trey asked, the disdain in his voice all too clear.

"As to the team, if the starting players are good, then they have nothing to worry about. I just need to make sure the team is capitalizing on the talents available and not overlooking anyone who's worked hard and deserves more playing time. Sometimes, players can be amazing but have weaknesses, and the other team can capitalize on them. It's my job to make sure when the situation presents itself, we eliminate that opportunity to give us the best shot at winning."

"Makes sense, I guess. But what about Gabby? A girl on the team will look bad."

"That's not true. If she makes the team, it's because she's as good as the boys already on it. And if she's that good, why wouldn't we want her? Could be a good thing for the Legal Eagles."

"Whatever. There's no way she'll make it, so I guess it's not a problem. She'll probably go home in tears, just like her mother with the snake." Trey smirked.

"Knock it off, Trey. Be nice. And keep me posted about anything I need to know from within the team. I need you as my wingman. I've got to go keep pace with some of the others."

"Gotcha," Trey confirmed, a sudden light in his eyes. If Connor hadn't been looking at his son, he would have missed it. *He needs you, not your trophies.* Lynette's words came to mind and Connor realized she might be right. A kid needed to be able to look up to his father. Someone who could be a role model to show what dreaming and hard work could produce in someone's life.

Connor dropped back, trying to talk to each of the kids, hoping to get a feel for their mindset. Not only about the game, but about life. Gabby was the last one in team A, and he pulled alongside her.

"Getting winded?" he asked.

"Yes, sir. A little. It's been a couple of months since I worked out. Sorry, Coach. Give me a week, and I'll be back in shape."

He liked her attitude, but it wouldn't help her now. "A week, huh? That's high aspirations and today's your one and only tryout."

"No, sir, not high aspirations. Fact. And being winded won't affect my other skills, trust me," Gabby said with a grin, even though her breaths were coming heavy.

"So why do you want to join the team mid-season? Why not just wait for next January and try out then?" he asked, curious how she would answer. It certainly would have been the easier route, and he admired her gumption.

"Idle players slide backward. I've been idle long enough."

No truer words could have been spoken. The girl had dedication and heart for the game. More than some of the other players he'd already spoken with. He couldn't wait to discover if there was any truth to her words because the team needed a good back-up pitcher, and no one else he talked with seemed to be overly interested. But then, he still needed to talk with the B team players. Hopefully, her words and actions added up to a winning player. In his experience, the two were far too often not in sync.

"Good enough. Show me what you got, and if the Legal Eagles need it, I'll find you a spot." The truth of the matter surprised him—a girl on the team something he'd never considered.

"Promise?" she asked with hope in her voice.

"I promise." The team might not like it, but he'd do what he could for Gabby *if* she was any good. The girl had been through a lot and needed someone to show her life wasn't all bad. The same could be said for Trey.

Something he'd do well to remember.

"Okay, let's bring it in," Connor hollered, blowing his whistle. Everyone came running, huffing and puffing. It would seem Gabby wasn't the only one not in the greatest of shape. Endurance was something he'd have to work on.

"What's next, Coach?" Timothy Adkins, one of the kids asked.

"Let's put Team A up to bat, Team B outfield. Riley, you're listed as the pitcher. Who else likes to pitch? My understanding is the relief pitcher moved away." Connor looked around the group to see who would step up. It was not an easy position and came with a lot of pressure.

Barry's been our relief pitcher since Art left," Riley said, speaking up for the boy when he said nothing. "We don't have anyone else." Connor looked over at Barry, who was, in turn looking at the ground. Not a lot of confidence...which was more than a little problem.

"I pitch," Gabby said confidently, stepping forward. Connor already knew it, and now, the whole team did. He steeled himself for their reaction.

"A girl? This ain't slow pitch, sister. Go back to softball," Riley said, joining in the laughter with the others.

"Whatever," Gabby said defensively.

Riley rolled his eyes, looking to his friends for backup.

Lynette stepped forward as if she was going to put an end to the debate.

The last thing Connor wanted was for someone to usurp his position and authority with the team. He drew in a deep breath and exhaled. "I guess there's only one way to settle this. Gabby, I was going to pitch first, but I think we need to mix things up a bit. You okay with pitching to the A-team?" He might as well find out the level of her abilities right away, as well using the opportunity to help the team become more settled having her around. *It could also put an early end to any chance she had to make the team.*

"Yes, sir. No problem," she said, a snide grin on her face entirely directed at Riley. "Watch and learn." She picked up a ball and headed for the pitcher's mound, glove in hand and ready for action. Gabby certainly had the right attitude—*own it.*

"Riley, why don't you lead us off and hit?" It was the best way to settle the score between the two kids. Otherwise, the animosity could get out of control and divide the team. He hoped for Gabby's sake, she could pitch.

Riley took his place, his stance low and wide. He settled his grip on the bat. "Let it rip, sister," he taunted.

Gabby stared him down a few seconds, wound up, and pitched a fastball. The ball sailed toward home plate with astonishing speed and accuracy, surprising even Connor. "Strike one," he called out.

"It was high," Riley challenged, a scowl on his face.

"Not on my watch. And if you have a problem with my calls, you're going to have a problem on this team." Connor wasn't about to let the kid get away with arguing with him. It would only translate down the road to arguing with an ump, something that would get Riley ejected from the game.

Riley lifted his bat, keeping his mouth shut. Tight, but silent.

Gabby wound up and pitched again, much the same as the first.

"Strike two," Connor called.

Riley glared at him but didn't say a word. The kid was a fast learner.

The third pitch came in hot and spot-on, but it was another fastball. This time Riley read the pitch and connected with the ball. They all watched as it flew over the head of the second baseman and landed in between two outfielders. In a game, the hit would have been easily worth a single, possibly a double.

"Good hit, Riley," Connor said.

The boy lifted his hat to the pitcher and bowed, rubbing the hit in. He returned to the dugout, a huge grin on his face as he and the other boys high-fived each other. "She got lucky the first two pitches. Show her how it's done, Devon," Riley shouted as the next batter walked up to the plate.

Connor would work on team spirit and attitude, but he wouldn't press his luck on the first day. What they needed to remember was they were still a team. Three pitches later, Devon had struck out. At that moment, Connor knew Gabby's fate with regards to the team. He'd have to work with her some on changing up her pitches, but the girl knew her stuff.

Trey came up to the plate. He settled in, his stance wide, hands choked up slightly on the bat. Gabby pitched. Trey swung and missed.

"Strike one," Connor called out. "Stay balanced on the balls of your feet, Trey."

Gabby pitched a knuckleball and it went high and left. His son managed to hit it, but the ball tipped off the bat and flew up and backward into the backstop. "Strike two."

The third pitch came in as a clean, fastball, but nowhere near the speed of the earlier ones. Trey connected with the ball solidly, crushing it. His son made a show of running the bases, taking a bow as he reached the dugout.

"Well done, Trey. That would be a contender for a home run judging by the distance you carried," Connor said. The kid was a chip off the old block, and a sense of pride filled Connor. Coaching Trey gave him a rush of excitement he hadn't known would happen.

"Thanks, Dad. It felt good." Trey walked closer to him. "And," he said, lowering his voice, "as much as I hate to admit it, Gabby *can* pitch. She's surprisingly good for a girl."

Connor was pleased his son had noticed the same thing he had and that he was willing to admit it out loud. "I agree. Not the girl part; she's as good as any boy her age, or better. Perhaps you could help some of the others adjust to her being on the team."

"She's in then?" Trey asked, not overly surprised.

"I don't see why not. Do you?"

Trey shook his head. "Reckon not." His approval would go a long way toward Gabby's acceptance on the team.

The rest of the practice went smoothly. Lynette had helped in any way she could but she stayed out of the official coaching arena. It had been more fun than Connor expected, and the bonding with Trey felt right. He'd do what he could to help the team, and by way of extension, Gabby and Trey. He wasn't a magician, but this team had potential, and with a little work and team spirit, they could be better.

The only problem as he could see it, would be Lynette's presence. When he'd agreed to let her help, he'd forgotten one important fact. A few of the other teachers had no qualms dropping some not-so-subtle comments about Connor's camping weekend with the new principal. No one seemed to remember it was unavoidable, instead, linking them together as a couple.

Something the Hallbrook gossip chain feasted on for excitement.

Chapter Ten

♥

A WEEK PASSED, WITH Gabby and Lynette both settling into the new routine at school. Thanks to Connor's open-mindedness about allowing Gabby on the baseball team, her daughter's mood had shifted to a more positive note.

Lynette watched as the kids packed up the gear. "Thanks, Connor. That was a productive practice, and some of your team-building exercises seemed to be paying off." She pointed at the group of boys walking off the field toward the parking lot, laughing and joking. And with Gabby. Like they were all part of something bigger than themselves and liked it.

Connor gathered the last of the supplies and shoved them in a bag, slinging it over his shoulder. "No thanks required," he said, joining her, the two of them heading for the car where Gabby and Trey waited.

A few of the boys hadn't come around to having Gabby on the team. Given time and a few games under their belts, Lynette hoped their attitudes would change for the better. Winning the last game had gone a long way to moving the team in the right direction, and they were in contention for the finals.

Something that hadn't gone unnoticed by anyone on the team.

Moving around hadn't allowed time for Lynette and her daughter to develop lasting friendships. For Gabby's sake, she hoped things would be different here in Hallbrook. At least they were off to a good start. They both were, for that matter. Her friendship with Connor was for the lack of a better word, nice. And by the looks of things, he'd be the one doing the leaving, but still, it felt good to make a friend.

"The kids look up to you. You're a hero in their books, and it shows in the effort they put into getting better, pulling together as a team." After the first practice, Connor had moved some players around and made a few other changes, and his perceptions were paying off.

"Well, I don't know if that's why, considering I've never made it to the majors. I'm not some big hotshot ballplayer. But they are a good group of kids, and I'm glad you made me do this." He grinned.

Lynette shook her head and smiled. "I didn't force you into this. Strongly suggested, but there was no force used. And the fact is, you made it to the minors by chasing your dreams. That's what these kids need to see. The rest, you and I both know is great coaching, opportunity, a little luck, and some dynamite genetics that make you a superstar." She opened the tailgate for Connor and stepped back out of the way.

He tossed the bags in the bed of the truck. "Wow, that's kind of depressing. Clearly, I didn't manage either one of those things—luck or genetics."

"Maybe not yet, but you said you're still trying," Lynette said, wishing she could take back her comment.

Connor leaned against the side of the truck, striking a casual pose with his hands in his pockets. "Which means I'm banking on luck? I'm not sure

I like that idea much. I've worked hard at this. Deserve this."

"I'm sure you do. But there are hundreds of other ballplayers thinking the same thing. You couldn't foresee the injury that took you out of the running or a divorce that prompted you to be a full-time parent. What you can do is embrace the future you've been given and find a way to make it your dream. Combine what you love." She hadn't meant to go down this path with Connor. Her life was hers to manage, and she should have learned by now to stay out of others.

"Is that what you're doing, Miss Ann Landers?" Connor chuckled. The corners of his eyes crinkled when he smiled, softening his expression. Charming was a good word for the man—when he wanted to be.

But at least he wasn't upset she'd crossed any boundaries. "I'm trying. I love working with the kids, and I've found a way to do it without all the chaos. What's wrong with that?"

"It's not like chaos was your dream, so it's not the same thing."

Lynette bristled at the implication. "My marriage to Dirk was supposed to be a dream—the happily-ever-after kind. I'd say I'm out of the running for that."

"I'm sorry. I shouldn't have said what I said." Connor shoved off from the truck, rubbing the back of his neck.

"Maybe not, but I can see why you did. I am trying to make the best of the hand life has dealt me. Maybe you should do the same instead of running away." If he could dish out advice, so could she. Lynette didn't know how the conversation had turned so serious, but it left her unsettled and wishing she was home.

"Who says I'm running?" Connor asked, his smile disappearing.

She shrugged. "Only you can decide that. What is it—"

"Come on, you two, everyone's meeting at Sally's for pizza," Trey hollered. "I'm riding with Tommy's parents."

Connor let out a deep breath. "We're coming. Meet you there."

Gabby was within earshot, and the conversation came to a dead end. "We really can't. I've got some things to catch up on for school," Lynette said, taking advantage of the opportunity to make a clean getaway.

"Mom, you can't do this. I need to be there. This isn't fair," Gabby cried out, hands on her hips.

Her daughter was right.

She was using work as an excuse to avoid Connor. It wasn't his fault she found herself watching him far more than she should. It wasn't his fault he could be irritating at times. And it wasn't his fault he wanted to still chase after his dream.

Her dream had ended, and Hallbrook was her new life. And part of that life was letting her daughter fit in. "Okay, I'll do my work tonight. See you there," she called out, waving to Trey and Connor.

They slid in the car, and Lynette started the engine.

"What were you two talking about? It was obvious to everyone that whatever it was—it wasn't good." Gabby eyed her with curiosity.

"Just grown-up stuff. Nothing serious." She smiled over at her daughter, trying to put her at ease. The last thing she wanted to do was heap more trouble on her shoulders.

"You didn't make Connor put me on the team, did you?" she asked as if the idea struck her suddenly, and it wasn't one she liked.

"Of course not. You are on the team based on talent. And I will say this, I don't think you could have gotten a better pitching coach anywhere. You could learn a lot from Connor, maybe enough for a scholarship to the college of your choice." Lynette couldn't imagine where Gabby would come up with such an idea, and her daughter should know better. The same couldn't be said for some of the kids or their parents, and comments of that nature were bound to come up, even it wasn't true.

Gabby rolled her eyes. "Oh, Mom. I'm in seventh grade. Can I please just enjoy baseball without everything having to be about college?"

"Okay. Sorry. It's a mom thing, but I understand." Kids didn't want to hear about more schooling at this age, but as a mother, she'd be remiss if she wasn't trying to pave the way for her daughter's future.

And find a way to pay for the paving.

They pulled into a parking spot close to the diner. The team was already inside, the noise volume on high. Only a handful of customers were seated at some of the other tables. Lynette couldn't help but notice the disdainful glares of some of the older customers as she glanced around. Not everyone wanted to deal with the high energy level of fifteen kids.

"Mom, I'm going to sit over here with some of the others. Hope you don't mind?"

Lynette hadn't thought this part through before agreeing. "No, go ahead." What she really wanted to say was *no, sit with me.*

One of the boys slid out of the booth at Connor's table as they approached. "Here, Principal Taylor, take my seat. I want to talk to Trey." The red leather seat was well-worn and cracked, but then the place looked like they'd been in business a long time, possibly even back to when the town was first founded.

With no choice, she took a seat, much preferring adult conversation to the animated chatter of the kids. "Thanks," Lynette said, taking his place. The boy next to Connor slid out of his seat and bounded off to join some of the others. "Was it something

I said?" she asked, using humor to cover the awkwardness. She was well aware of the conversation vacated only ten minutes earlier, and fairly certain neither of them would want to go down that avenue again to finish it.

Connor smiled. "I think it's more a case of adults versus kids."

"Then you should fit right in with them," Lynette said, the comment slipping out before she could stop it.

He looked at her in surprise. "Ouch. Is that how you see me? An overgrown kid? Not very flattering."

Lynette shook her head. "I'm sorry, that didn't come out the way I meant it. And not really. It's just that sometimes when you're out there with the kids, you seemed to become one with them. It's amazing to watch the connection." She needed to think before speaking if she wanted to keep her new friend.

"It's nice to know there's at least one thing about me you like." His teasing smile was back in place, causing her heart to do a somersault.

"I'd say there's more than one thing, Connor. You're better at fishing for catfish and bass than compliments, so I'm not saying another word." Most certainly not about his long, dark lashes or warm chocolate eyes. Up close like this, she could see every feature of his face in detail—and the man was downright handsome.

"It'll be a boring pizza party if you don't talk." He leaned back against the seat, sprawling his legs out under the table and bumping up against hers.

She pulled her feet back and to the other side to make room. "You know what I mean."

"I do," he teased. "I just like to make you laugh. I reckon you need more laughter in your life."

Lynette wanted to take offense, but the truth was—Connor was right. And he'd been more than gracious to forgive and forget their earlier conversation. "Maybe." One word that spoke volumes.

"Here you go," an older woman said, carrying several boxes of pizza, followed by another younger girl carrying even more boxes.

"Thanks, Sally. We'll just take one of the cheese pizzas and let the kids choose from the other boxes if you don't mind sorting through the requests."

"No problem. I'll just put them all over on this table and let Christina work out the particulars."

"Sounds great," Connor said, opening the box the woman handed him.

Lynette's stomach rumbled, the mouth-watering aroma of melted cheese, tomato sauce, and fresh herbs greeting her. The cheese was perfectly browned and lightly crusted, just the way she liked her pizza. More gurgling noises reminded her that she hadn't eaten much for breakfast. She took a slice and bit into it, careful not to burn the roof of her mouth. "*Hmmm*, this is good."

Connor put two slices on his plate. "I agree. I've been all over the country with the minor league, but so far, I've not found a pizza that compares to Sally's. Something in the spices, I reckon. That woman sure knows her way around a kitchen."

"Some things are best enjoyed and not explained." Lynette grinned. The same could be said for a lot of things in life—like her friendship with Connor.

He laughed. "Amen to that."

His comment took her by surprise. Not that anything shouted out *I'm not a believer*. It was just

she hadn't put that together as part of his character—an important part in her books. "Is that a clue
to the status of your soul? Praying, that is. Do you
go to church on Sundays?" Lynette asked, curious
how he'd answer.

"The church of baseball." Connor grinned and
took another bite of pizza.

Lynette, on the other hand, set hers down on the
plate. "You know, you could take Trey to church
on Sunday. I'm planning on attending and taking
Gabby to meet some of the kids in the youth group.
Not that I'm suggesting we go together or anything
like that," she added, trying not to send mixed messages that would strain their friendship any more
than she had already.

Connor frowned. "Honestly, I've never had the
time or thought about it much. Guess I could go."
He rubbed his hand across the back of his neck,
something he did quite often when he was mulling
over an idea. "Why don't I pick you up at eight? We
could grab some breakfast and then head over to
listen to Pastor Richard."

It was as though he'd completely missed that part
of her comment, or he was ignoring it. Either way,

it wasn't a good idea. "Or we could go separate and not give the town more to talk about than they already have."

"You're no fun," Connor said, shooting her a wink.

"That's what I've been told. But it works for me," Lynette added.

Connor shook his head and reached for her hand. "I wasn't serious."

She pulled away. "Dirk was. He certainly told me often enough. The problem was, he was the good-time boy who saw rainbows with each new station we transferred to. I saw the constant changes differently. I was left to set up a new house, get settled, start a new life, only to pack up and do it again. I'll take boring now if it means stability." She wasn't looking for a pity party from Connor.

"I see your point. Darlene felt the exact opposite. She hated being left behind after Trey was born and found it boring. But then she had an ulterior motive that had nothing to do with me. She just wanted the social status, and her complaining was mostly because I wasn't trying hard enough in her eyes. She found it all too easy to walk away from everything—including Trey."

"Maybe she'll come around. You never know. Given time she might miss her son and reach out to renew the connection." Lynette wasn't so sure it was true, as much as it was to give him hope—a hope he might pass on to Trey. Her heart was breaking for the young boy.

"It was just another failure. I should have tried harder with the club like Darlene said. And done more when I was home. I don't know—something. But then, come to think of it, she left for another ballplayer," Connor said, his voice taking on an edge.

"What do you think changed?" Lynette asked.

Connor scowled. "Aside from finding a way to ditch responsibility for her son, the new guy is in the major leagues. Someone who could fulfill her socialite dreams." There was so much anger in his words, and yet, he was doing his best to hold it all together.

Lynette reached for his hand. "I'm sorry. That must have hurt. It certainly doesn't speak highly of your ex," she said, lowering her voice to a soft pitch.

His gaze stayed fixated on their joined hands. "No, it doesn't. It also doesn't speak highly of my abilities. Maybe if I'd have made it to the majors, we'd still be together."

He was taking all the blame for a failed career and a failed marriage. The combination couldn't be healthy. "And maybe, the marriage wasn't meant to be," Lynette said, trying to ease his pain.

Connor's gaze drifted to her face, his shoulders dropping slightly as if he were tired. "You're probably right. We jumped into marriage while we were in college. We thought if we were more settled, it would look good to the scouts instead of looking like some wet-behind-the-ears kid coming out of school. It backfired when she got pregnant. That part wasn't in her plans. I'm hoping my next shot at tryouts will fix everything for Trey and me."

No wonder he wasn't ready to give up on his dreams. "What's so special about the next set of tryouts?" Lynette asked.

"It'll be my last shot. After that, I'll have aged out. Too many younger guys coming in with better arms, fancy moves, and a load of charm. I'll just be the old guy."

"You're not old. Not even close. And those younger guys don't have a lock on the charming market. You have your own charming side." The fact she was still holding his hand made the comment more interesting. And dangerous. It was borderline flirting.

Connor smiled. "Just one side, huh? I'll make sure to keep that side facing you."

Nothing borderline about what they were doing. She pulled her hand back, realizing she'd gone too far. "What do you mean?" she asked, laughing to cover her discomfort.

His grin broadened, the corners of his eyes crinkling in the way she liked. "Right or left?" he asked. "Which side is my charming side?"

Lynette shook her head. "Okay, okay. All of you." The guy was incorrigible when he turned it on. "So what do you think of the team and our odds of making the finals?" she asked, trying to change the subject. None of the other parents or kids were within earshot, and it was a good time to find out.

"I think they've got a chance of making it into the playoffs. We've only got a few more practices, but with the effort they are putting into this—anything's possible. Capitalizing on the talent pool is helping, and these kids are good."

Lynette let out a deep breath. It was just as she suspected. Connor was doing good things with the team, but what would happen if the team did make it to the playoffs and their coach was suddenly missing in action? It was a sobering thought.

"Why the long face? I thought I was giving good news and shedding hope on their prospects."

She nodded. "You are. I just hope you're here long enough to see it happen." It was the truth, even if she shouldn't have brought it up.

"I want to be, trust me. I also need to be realistic. I don't know the future, but while I'm here, I'm giving them everything I've got to help them succeed."

"I know you are." The thought of Connor staying in town set her heart to racing. They were friends, and friends supported one another in their dreams.

With the pizza all gone, the group got ready to leave. Connor settled the bill, picking up the entire tab. More proof of what a great guy he was, even if he couldn't see the truth.

"I'm going to the ladies' room. I'll be right back." She headed for the back area, finding it easier to breathe away from Connor. She was doing way too much thinking of him, considering the guy couldn't wait to leave town.

After washing her hands, she headed out of the restroom. Lost deep in thought, she ran smack dab into the hard wall of a chest. "I'm so sor—" The words wouldn't come as she recognized the chocolate brown eyes of her victim.

Connor.

"I'm not," he said in a husky voice meant only for her to hear. Seconds passed, neither one moving.

"Lynette…"

"Connor…" They both spoke at the same time.

"You go first," she said, still finding it hard to speak and needing a little more time to recover as the adrenaline rushed through her body. The man smelled like woods and spice and everything nice.

Connor lowered his head as if he were going to tell her a secret, his breath warm on her face. "I'm not sure I know what to say. I'm more of an action guy, and right now, for some strange reason, I want to kiss you."

Her brain was tripping over his words, but her heart knew exactly what to say. "For some strange reason, I'm okay with that," Lynette said in a breathless voice she barely recognized.

Connor closed the distance between them, moving slowly as if to savor the moment.

"Really? *Ewww*, Mom," Gabby said from behind them.

They sprang apart.

"It's n...not what you think. I r...ran into Connor, that's all," Lynette stumbled over the words, trying to be coherent for her daughter. Talk about poor timing.

"Sure you did," Gabby said, not believing a word of Lynette's cover story.

"I did. Tell her, Connor," Lynette said, trying to enlist him to come to her aid.

"Sure, she did," he said, with a wink, putting a lie to her words. *Some help he was.*

Lynette shook her head and walked away, unwilling to say another word. Anything she said would only incriminate herself more.

If she stood any chance against Connor's charms, Lynette figured they just went out the window. She never really understood the "almost kiss" term, but now she did. The *almost* was the part that would leave her wanting to find out what it would have been like, and it would keep her thinking about the man.

And none of those thoughts would be centered on the fact he was one of her teachers at the school, *or* that she was his boss...and therefore, off-limits.

Chapter Eleven

♥

SWEAT DRIPPED DOWN CONNOR'S face as he pressed himself to work through the last ten pushups. One hundred. He collapsed to the floor of the gym, rolling over on his back and wiping his face with a towel. Now for a five-mile run, two hundred sit-ups, and thirty minutes at the batting cage to keep his shoulder loose.

And all before seven-thirty when he needed to pick Trey up for school. It was a good thing his son was used to taking care of himself in the mornings as it was the only time Connor could knock out the routine.

The email he'd gotten two days ago from the Red Sox minor league coach accepting him into the tryouts scheduled for Memorial Day weekend had resulted in the same gut-wrenching ache in his stomach as it had when he was younger. It was like starting out all over again. At least they were still willing to give him a shot at the team.

But two things kept his excitement from bubbling over. One, he hadn't told Lynette or the school team about the upcoming tryouts. He didn't know how to tell them, fearing the disappointment he'd see on their faces. He'd been enjoying his time with Lynette, Trey, Gabby, and the Legal Eagles. They gave him a sense of purpose that had been missing since his life had fallen apart.

And two, the Legal Eagles' final win on Saturday had pushed them into the semi-finals. Unfortunately, the games were also scheduled for Memorial Day weekend. The team might never forgive Connor for deserting them, but he didn't have a choice. This was his last shot at the dream.

Trey was excited and talked nonstop baseball, something Connor normally enjoyed. His son's conversations centered on the semi-finals—the next step in going for the gold, and Connor simply didn't have the heart to tell him he wouldn't be there for the game.

Going for the gold is what had driven Connor in the past, and Trey was catching the same fever—the one called success. He was proud of his son, the kid quite the ballplayer. His own father hadn't stuck around long enough to see Connor's achievements, and the last thing he wanted to do now was follow in his father's footsteps.

Second-guessing his moves didn't come naturally. It wouldn't change anything. His future already laid out before him, ready for the taking. Connor was stronger, faster, healthier, and throwing a curveball like nobody's business. There were no guarantees, but he felt positive this was his moment to shine.

He'd paid his dues. More than most. *Less than some.* Lynette once reminded him not everyone could make it to the majors, and on more than one occasion, her words of wisdom held more truth than he liked.

Was he foolish to live life trying to go back on the road with the minor league, always waiting for the call? Maybe his chance was over, having sailed into the sunset with his injury and the divorce. What if

Lynette was right and he needed to let go of the past and start living in the present?

It all sounded so simple, but it was anything but easy. The issue of tryouts loomed ahead, teasing him with the possibilities. Then there was the issue with Lynette. He liked her more than a little. And yet, while he and Trey had grown closer over the past couple of weeks, whenever they spent time around Lynette, his son's attitude changed for the worse—almost as though he resented the time the two of them spent time together.

And then there was the kiss—the one that didn't happen. The one that had been his first and last opportunity to kiss Lynette. Not that he hadn't thought of what it would have felt like, or what her pink gloss-covered lips would taste like. He'd gotten a whiff of strawberry, which seemed young and carefree for a woman who held such great power with the school administration and board. Connor wanted more than anything to find out if he was right.

On and on, he continued to run, his feet pounding the track around the school. Lynette would never accept a relationship with a guy on the road...not with her history. Kissing her would have been wrong. The last thing he wanted to do was send her the wrong message. But what if it was the right message and he was missing out on something that could provide greater happiness than baseball?

What was he thinking? The moment of insanity passed. *Focus. Focus.* His feet pounded out the new rhythm, forcing all his concentration into extracting every ounce of energy he had to push his body to the limit.

Sam Hill came running toward him, pulling alongside and keeping pace. "Good morning. Hard at it, I see," Sam said. They were friends in and out of school, although not close. The schedule Connor once kept hadn't allowed for deep friendships outside the minor league, and those players and admin officials came and went far too often for anything lasting.

"Morning, Sam. Got to keep pushing myself, just in case." It was no secret he wanted to get back to the thrill of the game, but no one knew his chance was just around the corner.

"Think you'll make it?"

"Who knows? Kids these days seem like they're coming up through the ranks younger and younger."

"Or maybe you're just getting older and older." Sam chuckled.

"There is that." Connor grinned, allowing a touch of humor in his response. The truth was, it was something he couldn't ignore, no matter how much the thought messed with his head.

"So what's up with you and the new principal?" Sam asked.

Connor glanced over at his friend. "Nothing. Why?" He didn't like the sudden turn in the conversation.

Sam shook his head. "Nothing is *not* the topic of discussion in the break room and on the playground."

The cryptic comment wasn't undecipherable. "You should know better than to listen to gossip."

"It's not gossip when you all camped together. Like a family, I might add. Now she's coaching the middle school baseball team with you—a team you previously refused to coach. I'd say they have some real grit in the discussion. I'm only bringing it up to warn you. Some of the others are wondering about special favors and the issue of non-biased voting with regards to school policies. Things of that nature."

Hallbrook needed something else to focus on. His non-relationship with Lynette wasn't any of their business. "That's their problem. Not mine. I may not even be here after next week." His big mouth had just stepped off into the deep end.

"Oh? Where you headed?" Sam eyed him with interest.

Connor wasn't about to disclose any more information than he just had before he told Lynette and the kids. "I was speaking in general. You know, in case the tryouts come around."

"Gotcha. But right now, it's you and Principal Taylor on the gossip wire."

"We were forced to spend time together at the camp when the dam broke. Trust me, it wasn't planned by any means. I'm tired of defending something I had no control over."

"I believe you. I'm just the messenger. They are watching you, so you need to watch your back, my friend."

There was no sense to continue arguing the matter. People would think what they wanted, no matter what he said or did. It was a good thing they couldn't read his mind considering he was still thinking about kissing Lynette. "Thanks. I know you mean well. I'll race you to the finish line. I've still got to head over to the batting cage before school starts."

"You're on." The two of them took off running, Connor pushing himself hard. Partly because he needed to, and partly to work off the anger fueled by the conversation.

They drew up short at the line, leaned over, both breathing hard as they tried to catch their breath. "Good sprint. I've got to keep running," Sam said while jogging in place. "See you at school," he called out as he took off once again.

"Later." Connor jogged back to the gym and grabbed his duffel bag. Batting practice would be cut short today, considering everything took longer than normal.

The grueling pace he kept was wearing him out, and it was a cause for concern. The young players at tryouts would have no such problem.

Connor watched as the last of the kids left, his son and Gabby having already disappeared with friends after practice. Lynette tossed the last of the duffel bags in the back of the truck.

He walked Lynette to her car. "Any interest in grabbing a bite to eat?" he asked, more than willing to ignore Sam's warning. Especially given that he had yet to tell her the truth, and he was leaving town after school tomorrow.

"I'm not sure it's a good idea. Not without the kids anyway," Lynette added.

Connor shook his head and smiled. "You wouldn't say that if you knew this town. Word is out that we are an item, and nothing we say is going to change that. Coaching together sealed the deal in their eyes after the camping trip."

Lynette huffed, crossing her arms in front of her chest. "That's ridiculous. I'm helping for Gabby and Trey and the other kids. And if what you're saying is true, the board will be calling me to task. Something I don't need." Judging by her answer, Lynette wasn't having the same problem he had when it came to thinking about the missed opportunity for a kiss.

"There are several couples working together at the school. Somehow, they all manage to figure out ways around the board and the problems. Maybe it's not such a big deal," Connor said, testing the waters. Something he shouldn't do but could no more stop himself, than he could stop from wondering about what it would be like to kiss her.

"Maybe, but we aren't a couple."

Connor stepped closer. "I realize that. But to be honest, I haven't stopped thinking about the other day. You know—when we almost kissed." They were two people who enjoyed an easy friendship, worked together, played together. Heck, they even both had kids who went to the same school. There wasn't any reason they shouldn't be together.

Well, all except the one—and it was a doozy. If he made the team, he'd be gone far more than he would be around.

Lynette grinned. "That's saying a lot. What with school, Trey, the middle school team, and your own career, I can't imagine you've had more than a few seconds to think about it," she teased.

"Now who's fishing for information?" he asked, moving closer.

"Hardly."

"Well, I have. And for way more than a few seconds. It may not make sense, but sometimes, the best things in life don't."

Lynette's eyes grew wide, her gaze softening. "Connor...I don't—"

He silenced her words with a kiss, slow and tender, until she responded. It would have been more proper to kiss her cheek and walk away, but he could no more resist her glossy lips than he could the call of baseball. Lynette closed her eyes, as if she too wanted to give in to the moment.

"This is just great, Dad," Trey said from behind them. "Kissing the principal. Seriously? What about Mom?"

Busted. Connor dropped his arms just as Lynette turned away, her focus suddenly on something in the backseat of her car.

He turned to face his son. "What about your mom? This has nothing to do with her. And I thought you left with Jerry?"

"I changed my mind and went to the bathroom. Thought you saw me head that way since you did wave," Trey said, the sarcasm in his voice all too revealing.

For some reason, his son had a serious problem with Lynette. "I was waving at one of the other parents and never saw you. Glad I hadn't left." It was easier to ignore the rest of the discussion.

Trey scowled. "I'm wishing you had. Then I wouldn't have to figure out how to unsee what I saw."

Connor wouldn't let him continue to be disrespectful, but it also wasn't a conversation he wanted in front of Lynette. "That's enough, son. We'll talk about it later."

"You kissed her. I would have thought you'd had enough of women and the problems they cause in our lives." There was so much anger in his voice it shook Connor to the core.

"Go get in the truck. I'll be right there." The conversation they needed to have was long overdue. And it was one they needed to have soon. Preferably before Connor left town.

Trey stormed off, the weight of the world on his shoulders.

"Sorry about that. He's been angry with his mother ever since she left. I'll talk to him," Connor said, trying to ease past the awkwardness. What he'd rather do was rewind to the kissing part and pretend Trey hadn't seen a thing.

"Don't worry about it. It was just a kiss between two friends. Nothing can come of it, and Trey will get over it eventually. Probably when we win the semi-finals game," Lynette said, smiling as she tried to infuse humor into the situation.

"I don't kiss my friends like that, but we can go your route for the time being. It'll make things easier in the short run."

"The time being? Short run?" she asked, her brow drawn tight.

"We can discuss it when I get back Monday. I've been meaning to tell you something, but the right moment hasn't come up," Connor said, knowing it was time to speak up.

"Tell me what?" Lynette tilted her head to one side as she waited for him to explain.

"I got an email from the league a couple days ago. They've approved me to attend tryouts as a special favor, considering my history with the team."

"That's wonderful news. I bet you're excited." Her smile was genuine, but it was one that wouldn't last when she heard the details.

"I would be more excited if it wasn't this weekend. I won't be able to coach the semi-finals game."

Lynette's eyes darkened in disbelief. "This weekend? But you can't go. The kids are counting on you," she said, shaking her head, unwilling to believe he'd leave.

"It's not like I have a choice. The minor leagues only have tryouts once a year. I need this. The kids will be fine—you'll see." *At least he hoped they would be.* The thought of leaving them in the lurch wasn't one he relished.

"How can you say that? And what about Trey? He'll be heartbroken. I'm sensing he may be upset with a whole lot more than you think. His mother deserted him, and now that's what you're going to do. When does it all stop, and you settle down? You're picking baseball over your son." It would have been better if Lynette had been yelling at him, but her passionate words were spoken with calm, matter-of-fact emotion.

"Spoken from someone whose dream is stability and family and having her shot at that life as we speak." Lynette was right, but at what point did she try to understand his needs counted also? How could anyone think he should simply fold the hand he'd been dealt and accept life the way it was? His happiness was tied to baseball. And if he was happy, his son would be happy. It made sense.

Lynette's nostrils flared, a deeper emotion coming to the surface when he turned the conversation toward her. "What's wrong with wanting a stable life filled with a love that comes from sharing and family?"

"Nothing, apparently. *For you.*" Connor started toward his truck, but paused, turning back. "I was hoping you could coach the game tomorrow. If not, I'll understand and try to find someone else."

"Of course, I will. Good old reliable Lynette," she added, her tone sarcastic. She got in her car and drove away without another word, leaving him standing there and watching her departure.

Connor knew he shouldn't have kissed her. Relationships, in general, were trouble. When would he learn?

But he'd been right...her lips tasted like strawberry.

Chapter Twelve

♥

LYNETTE HEADED FOR THE kitchen, Bingo following close behind. She was intent on tracking down her brother since he'd arrived back home last night. There was much to tell him, and hopefully, she could convince him to help her out with the Legal Eagles and the semi-finals game today.

She'd agreed to Connor's proposal to take over coaching the game in his absence, but the truth was she didn't know enough about the strategies he employed. In essence, she'd be winging it. For that matter, Trey could run the game better than she could—something she might have to resort to if her brother refused to help.

Connor left after school yesterday, and Trey had spent the night with her and Gabby. Technically, he was under Keith's care, but a delayed flight put

Lynette in the hot seat, trying to keep two young kids occupied and getting along. An adventure movie and popcorn did the trick, but even settling in on one movie had taken the better part of thirty minutes.

"Good morning, Keith. Nice to see you *finally* made it home." Her brother looked a little rough around the edges this morning, his five o'clock shadow leftover from yesterday now appearing more like several days of scruff. Judging by the half-empty pot of coffee, even caffeine wasn't helping him.

"Hello to you too, sis. It's been a rough month, so go easy on me. What a nightmare trying to get that plant back up and running. But they are all caught up on orders, and it's back to normal business." Keith topped off his coffee and sat down at the table, Bingo moving to sit next to him and nudge his arm in hopes of getting some attention.

Lynette poured herself a cup of the brew, skipping the instant coffee machine for once. Her brother had a knack for making coffee with just the right amount of freshly ground robust beans.

"Maybe. But you owe me a favor, and I know just how you can pay me back."

Keith cocked one eyebrow up. "First, why do I owe you a favor? You *are* staying in my house, rent-free I might add—not that I mind you here."

He had a point, but she needed him. Now wasn't the time to back down over minor points. "True. And I'm grateful to you for helping us out on the transition. I'm hoping to find a place soon, and we'll be out of your hair. But as to the favor, it's because you left Gabby with a stranger. I had to rush up here and then got stranded at the state park—camping of all things."

Keith frowned. "I left her with my best friend. Where's the problem? I still don't understand why you were so upset. It's not like I dumped her with some random guy."

"But Connor was a stranger to me. We've been over this before." Her brother simply didn't get it. He didn't understand the fear a parent faced, worrying something bad might happen to their children.

"At least three times if my memory serves me right. It's not my fault you didn't trust me and came rushing back here in a tizzy and tried to rescue her. I still can't believe you got stuck camping with Trey and Connor. I would have loved to see that." Keith grinned, confirming he found it funny, and not a serious issue the way she saw it.

"Stuck being the operative word, and why you owe me. I see it as all your fault," Lynette added, driving home her point.

Keith shook his head. "I disagree, but what is it you want me to do? It must be important, given the lead-in." Her brother stood, moving to the sink to rinse out his cup.

"Help me with today's baseball game. It's the semi-finals, and I promised Connor I'd take over, but I'm not sure I'm ready for this. The kids have come so far, and Connor's absence will upset them. I still can't believe he left like this. We need a strong role model to hype them up. If they win today, they're in the championship next weekend. It's a big deal. Far bigger than I'm ready to fly solo for." Lynette didn't want to let the kids down, and she wasn't beyond begging.

"Tough break on the timing, but surely, you un-derstand Connor had to leave. There will be other school baseball games, but it's his last chance to get back into the minors and perhaps even the majors. I do understand, however, that today's game is important to the kids." He stopped petting Bingo. The dog went back to nudging his arm until Keith relented and resumed the petting session. "Trey and Gabby are two good reasons to help, so yeah, I'll do it. All you had to do was ask without all the other nonsense."

Relief filled Lynette, knowing she wouldn't have to do a crash course in coaching before the game rolled around. "Thanks a lot. I really appreciate it. But I can't help but notice you left me out of your reasoning. Guess I don't count," she teased.

Keith grinned up at her. "You always count, but you're an adult and can fend for yourself. Clearly." The twinkle in his eyes revealed he was thinking of something far different than her as a responsible adult.

"What's that supposed to mean?" she asked.

His grin only widened, the dimples on his cheeks becoming deep pools. Devilish was the adage she remembered. "Well, I did hear how well you managed to escape a snake while kayaking. That ought to count for something." Keith laughed.

Lynette moved close enough to punch him in the shoulder, her brother ducking out of her reach. It had been a traumatic event, so having the guys making light of it didn't sit well. "Not funny."

Woof. Woof. Bingo wanted to join in the fun, and Lynette played with him, letting the dog chase her around the kitchen.

"So, what time is the game?" Keith asked, bringing the conversation back to what was important.

"Noon."

He nodded. "That doesn't give us much time. Can you handle calling all the kids or their parents and try getting them to the field an hour early? I've got something important I want to say and do with them. Motivational stuff. My specialty considering I just had a refresher course in motivating thousands of workers to increase output and hours. Successfully, I might add."

Her brother had always been good at motivational speeches, even in high school. It's what made him successful as a regional manager for Tek Foods, Inc. "Thanks. I was sure I could count on you if you made it back in time. Connor said he'd find someone else, but then that would have opened up an assortment of problems I wasn't willing to open." Some memories with Connor were ones she preferred to forget, others not so bad, but the staff at school were always angling for full disclosure and determined to have them admit to something that didn't exist. Would never exist, given Connor's new career status.

"What sort of problems?" he asked.

"I'm surprised Connor hasn't said anything to you, given the whole town thinks they know everything. They believe,Connor and I are a couple. With him leaving this weekend, a fill-in teacher would cause more questions, comments, and more speculation. The focus needs to remain on the kids and the game."

"Well, I'll be." Keith stroked his chin, nodding. "He didn't say a thing to me. But now that you mention it, I think you two would make a great couple."

"We aren't together. People just think we are." Well, maybe they were a little bit of an item. The kiss changed things, but then so did his departure.

Lynette wasn't settled about any part of her relationship with Connor, friend-wise or otherwise.

"But you could be. You're both single and with a kid in middle school. Sounds like a solid foundation for a relationship. Plus, he's my best friend, and you're my best sister."

"I'm your only sister," she retorted, unwilling to discuss the rest.

"True. Minor point." He shrugged, heading for the door. "Think about it, sis." She'd already thought about it far too often—more wouldn't help.

"You're forgetting, I'm his boss."

His boyish grin surfaced yet again, her brother having far too much fun with this. "Boss is just another word for making it interesting." Keith winked. "Now, get on that list...we don't have much time."

There was no use arguing the issue. Keith wasn't listening to a word she had to say about it. "Okay. Connor left all the equipment in the garage, so have at it."

"Great. We can meet at the fields with whoever can join us. I'll take Gabby and Trey with me." Her brother had gone into take-charge mode and would get the ball rolling.

Lynette let out a deep sigh of relief. Today would be a good day, thanks to her brother. She started calling the team's parents to get everyone on board. Before long, she had all but two of the kids arriving early. There wasn't any choice but to leave Bingo at home, the ballpark no place for the dog, especially with her attention tied up coaching. Trying to coach was more like it. As for her, she was more than willing to take a back seat to the action, the same way she did with Connor.

Keith, Gabby, and Trey were at the field when Lynette showed up. They were all gathered around in a team huddle. Her brother's voice grew clearer as she approached.

"This is about each and every one of you. You've worked hard to get here, and the school is proud of you. But most importantly, you should be proud of yourself. You've proven you have the right to be here, and that you have what it takes to win. When you go out on that field today, I want you to think of it like any other game. Have fun. Picture the other team in their underwear if you need to, anything to make you laugh and have fun. Loosen up. That's what is key here." Her brother's motivational speech was spot on, but the kids were slow to respond.

"It still stinks that Coach Weston isn't here. It would be cool if he makes the minors, but still, he should have been here." It was Gabby who spoke up, and several of the kids mumbled in agreement.

"Maybe so, but remember, this is what we all play for. The dream. It starts as fun, but at some point, it gets in your blood. And when it does, it drives your every decision. If any of you ever get the chance, you wouldn't turn your back on it either. Coach Weston spent his whole life chasing this dream. I say, instead of wishing he was here, let's pray he does his best and that when he comes home, it's to a trophy we can share with him. Let's make him proud," Keith said, his voice growing louder and more positive. Lynette got chills as she pictured the image her brother painted.

The kids all murmured in agreement, louder as their spirits lifted. Lynette smiled as she thought about all the times Keith had done the same for her when she was growing up. It wasn't until she married Dirk that her life became centered on someone else and revolved around his life—as though she ceased to matter.

"Let's get to it with a warm-up. Start by forming two lines and throw the ball back and forth to each other twenty times, and then sprint to the end of the field and back. Then do a repeat but throw ground balls," Keith called out.

The kids did as they were told, leaving Lynette an opportunity to watch the other team warm up, checking out the competition. The team was from Glen Haven, their closest neighbors. It would stir up rivalry for sure between the schools. More people arrived on the scene, Lynette noting the black and white striped jerseys. "Hey, Keith. It looks like the umps are here," she called out to alert him.

"Fall in, team," he hollered. "It's time to rock this win! Remember, this is for Coach Weston."

"Yay!" They all cheered, tossing their gloves in the air, catching them and making a beeline for the home field dugout. The kids were at an all-time-close camaraderie, something Connor had planted within them, and Keith managed to blossom right before the game.

The captains were called out while the others swung bats to stay loose. Riley and Gabby tossed a ball back and forth, keeping their arms warmed up. The buzz of activity was equaled only by the buzz of parents in the stands, both sides filled to standing room only.

It was disappointing Connor wasn't there, but Keith seemed to understand, and so should she. Just because they were in different places in life, didn't mean she couldn't cheer Connor on. And so far, she'd done nothing to bolster his confidence or show she wanted the best outcome—*for him*. After today's game, she needed to send him a text, showing her support—and hopefully with the picture of a winning scoreboard.

Riley took to the field as the leading pitcher, and luckily, Gabby understood the system. As the newcomer, she still had some proving ground and would work herself up to more playing time. She'd worked a lot with Connor, and her pitching had improved with a lot more variety of pitches. Lynette was unable to remember the names or know what they meant. To her, a slider was something she ate—mini sandwiches.

"Strike one," the ump called out, Riley delivering the ball right down the pocket.

Lynette handed out Gatorades to the kids, hoping to keep them hydrated. She'd worn black sweats and a t-shirt and was hot, but the kids in their jerseys had to be hotter. Or maybe they wouldn't notice, the thrill of the game superseding all else.

"Strike two," the ump called when the batter swung and missed.

"Good job, Riley," Lynette called out her encouragement. "Stay with it."

Riley looked to Keith for a signal on what pitch to throw, but the kid shook it off. Keith signaled again with the same response. Her brother took off his hat and turned away in frustration. The kid was on his own. No one had ever dared shake off Connor.

Riley got set into position and pulled back, pitching to the batter.

Crack. The batter connected with the ball, catching the full meat of it, and sent it sailing over third base and down the line, past the outfielder. By the time Andrew caught up with the ball and threw it in, the player had already rounded the bases and slid into home plate with ease.

Keith went out to talk to Riley. The kid didn't look happy, but the expressions of his teammates were equally unhappy. It was far too soon to lose faith.

Her brother came back, clapping his hands and cheering on the team. "It's just one, no big deal. Let's knock this inning out, one player at a time." He certainly had a way of staying cheerful and motivating.

At the end of five innings, the game was 7 - 7. Riley was still pitching, but it looked like he was tiring, and some of the other team's players had capitalized on his weakness. The rules were clear that every player had to be in the game for a minimum of two innings, and Keith had to rotate Gabby in.

Lynette prayed her daughter would do well for her sake and the team's sake.

"Pitching change," Keith said, holding up his hand to signal for a time out. "Gabby, you're in."

Her daughter couldn't have been more excited as she grabbed her glove and headed for the mound.

She warmed up with a few pitches and then settled in, signaling she was ready.

Her first three pitches were strikes, which then quickly turned into six strikes, and two outs. Her daughter was on a hot streak, plugging in some of Connor's moves he'd taught her. Even her posture on the mound had changed...now more determined, and her follow-through would allow Gabby to be ready to field the ball if necessary.

"Come on, honey, you can do it," Lynette called out, pacing back and forth, her nerves tightly wound.

"Strike one," the ump called.

Lynette couldn't breathe. Gabby was dialed in and focused.

"Strike two."

Lynette stopped, unable to do anything other than focus on Gabby. She almost wanted to close her eyes, but there was no way she wanted to miss the action. A shutout inning would be a miracle right here.

"Strike three," the ump called.

The Legal Eagles came running in, pumped and excited with Gabby's performance. It was just the boost they needed. They cheered her on, bumping shoulders like she was just one of the guys.

The batter rotation had landed on the pitcher as first up to bat. Her daughter needed more work on hitting, and she failed to connect with the ball, costing the Eagles their first out. Some of the excitement in her daughter's eyes dissipated.

The Thompson boy warmed up by swinging his bat and stepped up to the plate, ready to go. He swung and missed. Settling down a little lower at the plate, he swung at the next pitch and connected—a fly ball to the outfield that only got him a single.

They went through batter after batter, and when Devon took to the plate, he crushed the ball, bringing in the second run of the inning. By the bottom of the sixth, the score was 9 - 7, with the Eagles ahead. The top of the seventh inning brought more tension, the game too close to call. Middle school rules called for this to be the final inning of play, but in the case of a tie in a semi-finals game, they would go into extra innings. There could be only one winning team.

Adrenaline was riding high.

"Don't mess this up, Gabby. Everything is riding on you. You can't let them score."

Riley was getting into Gabby's head, but the last thing her daughter would want was for Lynette to step in to handle the situation. So, she did the only thing she could do—ignore the boy's mean comment and cheer her daughter on. "Come on, Gabby. You've got this." She cheered and clapped as her daughter took to the field.

The first batter stepped up to the plate. Gabby pitched right down the strike zone, and the kid swung, connecting solidly and making it to first base. Keith nodded encouragingly, trying to keep his niece in the mental game of pitching, knowing this would have shaken her up badly. It was a lot of pressure.

"Strike one," the ump called.

Gabby pitched another, her stance not as low, her pitch not as confident. The batter swung and connected, managing a double. The slump of Gabby's shoulders told her all she needed to know. Her daughter was thinking she was going to cost the team the game, ending their shot at the championship. A loss here, and the season was over.

The next batter struck out. The next hit a triple and three runs were scored.

A 10 - 9 ball game, the Legal Eagles were now behind. Gabby was tense, and her throwing reflected it. Luckily they were at the bottom of the roster and the last two batters struck out, ending the top of the seventh.

The Legal Eagles were quiet as they came into the dugout, knowing what was at stake.

"You really messed that up royally, Gabby," Riley said, a sneer on his face.

"Leave her alone. She's not the whole team, and it takes a team to win. You let the other team score seven, so your track record with them isn't anything to brag about," Trey said, defending Gabby.

Her daughter looked up at Trey in shock, as did Lynette. She hadn't known the two had become friends through all the issues that started from when they first were at odds during the camping trip.

"Sorry, I got nervous," Gabby said, her shoulders slumped, the defeat echoed in her eyes.

Trey shook his head. "Who wouldn't with Riley breathing down your neck."

Riley scuffed the ground with his foot and walked off to the side.

"Remember everyone, this is a team. If we win, we win as a team. If we lose, we lose as a team," Trey said, addressing the rest of the kids. Connor would have been proud of his son at this moment, making her wish even more he hadn't missed out.

The first two batters struck out. Tommy managed to hit a single and get on base, keeping the game alive. Trey stepped up to the plate. The tying run was on first, the winning run at the plate.

Lynette said a small prayer for Trey. He was a good kid. Mad at life but still managing to hold it all together. He swung the bat and pulled two strikes. The third splintered the bat as it connected, the ball sailing through the air, high and long out into the outfield.

"Run, run, run!" Keith yelled, motioning for the runners to keep going. Tommy cleared home plate with Trey right on his heels. The ball was thrown in just as Trey got there. He slid into home plate, trying to avoid the catcher's mitt.

"Safe!" the ump called, flailing his arms to signal to the crowd.

He'd done it. Trey just scored the winning home run. The Legal Eagles were going to the championship game. She ran forward to hug the boy, getting in line behind Keith and an excited group of kids. They lifted Trey onto their shoulders and carried him to the dugout. With laughter and cheering, the team celebrated the win.

Keith settled them down long enough to have them form a line and return to the field, doing the traditional good-game routine with the other team, showing sportsmanship.

"BBQ at my house to celebrate," Keith called out. Parents and kids alike were as excited as could be as they all headed for the parking lot. "Let's meet in an hour to give me time to stop at the Piggly Wiggly and grab some hotdogs and burgers and all the fixings." That was a lot of food, but Keith was in his element. This Memorial Day weekend wasn't one they would soon forget.

Trey hung back, and Lynette fell in step next to him. For a kid who just scored the winning run, he wasn't overly excited. "What's bothering you? You should be happy and full of smiles and with the others celebrating your victory."

Trey shook his head. "Honestly, I wish my Dad could have been here to see it." The dejected set of his shoulders spoke volumes. "I'll get over it, just like I always do, but you asked, so I answered."

Lynette was surprised by his admission, especially given his attitude toward her in the past. It made her want to give him a hug and wipe away his hurt. "I'm sorry, Trey. Your father was in a difficult position. I know he was upset that that he had to miss your game. Given how the game finished, he'll be doubly upset. Hopefully, someone caught it on video, and you can share the moment with him that way."

"It's not the same thing. And everyone else on the team had a mom or a dad here, cheering them on. Not me," Trey said, his voice dropping lower.

A kid needed a parent to support them and show they cared, and the fact Trey had been the only one on the team without someone hadn't crossed her mind. "He'll be back soon, and then you can tell him all about it. Look at it as a way to relive the moment and enjoy the glory longer." She was grasping at straws to find the right words. This was a moment in his life he would never forget, and she wanted it to be a happy one.

Trey stopped walking and looked up at her. "And then what? If he makes it, he'll be gone again."

The kid had a point. "Deal with that when and if it happens. There's no sense in borrowing trouble until you know for sure. Besides, I'll be here cheering you on," she said, ruffling the boy's hair.

Trey shook his head. "You know, for a principal, you're not half bad."

"I'll take that as a compliment," she said, smiling at him. "Have you ever told your dad how you feel? About him being gone and all?"

"No. All he ever talks about is getting back in the minors for another shot at the majors. And I mean, I want him to make it. It's cool. It's just...well, I want him here for me, too. Is that wrong?"

Lynette pondered the question, searching for the right words. "Not at all. I'd say it's normal—and quite mature. I think you should talk to your dad. The two of you could try and work something out. I don't know the answers, but neither will you unless you try."

And maybe she should take her own advice and talk to Connor. After the kiss, she'd been confused. They were close, but she wasn't sure it was enough for her, what with his dreams of coming and going and following a baseball team. It wasn't the life for Gabby—*or her*.

Lately, however, Lynette wasn't so sure about that either because she'd noticed when her daughter worked with Connor, she'd grown attached to her coach. More than as a coach, she wondered if Gabby wasn't looking up to him more as a father figure.

It was entirely possible, but an idea that was rife with problems.

Chapter Thirteen

♥

A WIN. THE LEGAL Eagles had pulled it off, and they were headed for the championship game next weekend. Connor had listened to the game on the radio headset in between the tryout drills. He was proud of his son and more than ever wished he'd been there.

Instead, he'd been stuck in Boston for two days of grueling tryouts. All around him, there had been young men who were fit, hyped up, and eager for the call. Guys much like him—ten years ago. Guys he had nothing in common with other than baseball. Their jokes and stories about parties and women held no interest for Connor. Listening to the game had given him a great excuse to bow out of the trash-talking conversations, at least for a few hours.

And in the end, tryouts were over, and Connor was headed home. He'd done everything he could, but he had been realistic enough to know his best wouldn't be enough. When the cut list had been sent around, it was no surprise his name had been crossed out.

The next generation of ballplayers had moved into the limelight, and they were hungry for the spots that would open on the roster. Connor's pitching had been on point—solid and reliable. But that's where his skills ended. One guy had all that and more. *Way more*. Fastballs. Curves. Sliders. Sinkers. You name it—and the one thing that set him apart from the others was the way he threw with heart. Every pitch flew from his fingertips like poetry. Enough so, Connor had even commented on it to one of the coaches. The kid was going places—it was written in the baseball stars. *The same stars Lynette had mentioned.*

Heading home, Connor was anxious to get back to Hallbrook. And Trey. He had a lot of making up to do with his son—his heart heavy with regret. The moment the announcer called out the play, it had sent chills down his spine, picturing his son's glory.

It was a memory they'd never completely share. And for what? Chasing dreams.

At least all that was about to change. He'd been cut, and that part of his life was over. *Officially*. Hallbrook was his new life, and the best part was, he'd be at the school's championship game. Be where he needed to be for Trey. They'd never be able to recapture the game he'd already missed, but there would be plenty more in the future.

The ride home gave him the time needed to collect his thoughts and put his dreams in a locked box. Now it was time to refocus and figure out the next part of his life. It was heart-wrenching, but a little soul searching had him in the right frame of mind by the time he passed the town's welcome sign.

He pulled up to the house and slid out of the car. Connor considered hiding out for a bit, unsure if he was ready to face the others and admit his failure, not wanting to see disappointment written on the faces of the people he cared the most about.

On the upside, staying in Hallbrook would give him a shot at developing the relationship with Lynette. She'd wanted him to walk away from baseball and to focus on his future and Trey. Well, she was getting exactly what she wanted for his life. That should count for something.

Trey, on the other hand, would have his father around more. Again, he'd be a failure in his son's eyes, but there would be some consolation. Especially given he would be here to coach the championship game.

With any luck, they'd have a win to share.

Trey's win. The Legal Eagle's win. *Not his.*

Connor turned and headed for Keith's place, ready to get it over with.

Lynette stepped off the front porch, her smiling face a burst of sunshine. "Hey, stranger. I thought I saw you pull into the driveway."

Dressed in jeans and a button-down dress shirt, she looked casual and comfortable. Closer to the way he remembered her at practices and games—the real deal. Not the starchy-suited principal at school trying to present an authoritative image. "Hi. I just got back and was trying to decide whether to unload first or check in with everyone." It was close enough to the truth. Now that the moment was upon him, part of him wished he'd chosen to unload. Anything to delay the inevitable of admitting his failure.

"Trey is anxious to see you. We all are. You haven't said a thing in your messages, and of course, he wants to tell you all about the game. It was incredible. But tell me, how did it go with you? When will you find out if you made it?" she asked, her voice light and refreshing after spending a weekend with a bunch of young guys who hadn't learned how to talk about anything other than baseball.

Connor shoved his hands in his pockets, steeling himself for her reaction. "I already know."

"Oh," she said, the smile slipping from her face. "You don't seem overly excited, so I'm guessing you didn't make it. I'm so sorry, Connor. I know how much you wanted this." She stepped closer, reaching out to touch his arm.

The sympathetic gesture was his undoing. Either that, or it was her touch. "You guessed right." He shrugged. "I did want it, but it doesn't seem as though it was meant to be. I've decided to put it all behind me and do what you said—settle down. Make a life here with Trey." He waited for the disappointment to show on her face, or for Lynette to pull away in disgust.

"Really?" she asked, her eyes taking on a light that said she was anything but disappointed in him.

He'd been so worried about her and Trey's reaction, he'd missed something important. Lynette cared about him, and not for his baseball skills She was nothing like his ex-wife. "Really." Connor reached out to take her hand, clasping them together as he pulled her closer. "I'm also hoping that based on the kiss we shared, you'll give me a chance as well. You know, like in a relationship. I'm here to stay, and I know how much you crave stability. It's something I can offer you now."

Lynette's smile matched the twinkle in her eyes. "Oh. I'd like that, and I know how much Gabby looks up to you."

Connor needed more from her. He needed to hear the words to confirm what he only suspected at this point. They needed an honest relationship if they were going down this road, something he hadn't had the first time around. "So you'd say yes for Gabby? What about you?"

Lynette blushed. "For me, too. I care about you. More than I should, given the circumstances. Speaking of which, what are we going to do about work? It still presents a problem with the school board watching our every move." Her thumb brushed against the back of his hand nervously.

"It's only a problem if we let them browbeat us over it. When it comes to decisions that need to be made, if there's a conflict of interest, one of us will bow out. More than likely, me."

"You make it sound so easy." She tried to take a step back, but he wouldn't let her go. Not after she'd already admitted she cared.

"What's really bothering you?" he asked.

Lynette let out a deep sigh. "I don't want to be your second choice in life, and that's what this feels like. You're back in Hallbrook because you didn't make the team. If you had, we wouldn't be having this conversation. Around here, that's called the second choice."

Connor tilted her chin up, losing himself in the depths of her blue eyes. "I'm sorry. I had to try. I hope you can understand what it meant to me. But it's over. That part of my life is closed, and

I'm starting fresh. Here in Hallbrook and hopefully with you. I can promise you this, whatever I do here, comes first. Just say yes, and it starts right now—with us."

Lynette remained silent for what he could only term awfully long seconds. "Yes. I'm willing to give this a shot. Us." Her radiant smile was back in place.

Connor said a silent prayer of thanks, knowing he'd been given a gift from God. "Good." He pulled her closer and lowered his head to claim her mouth in a kiss. Warm and welcoming—he was home.

"What is it with you two? Every time I see you, you're kissing," Gabby said, standing there with her hands on her hips.

"Don't exaggerate," Lynette said. "It was a welcome-home kiss. He's here to stay."

Gabby's gaze slid to their locked hands. "To stay? Does that mean—"

Connor nodded. "I didn't make the team." Saying the words the second time came easier. He'd be repeating them a lot the next few days, so it was a good thing.

Gabby's smile reminded him of her mother. "I know this sounds bad, but I'm glad. Now you can keep helping me with my pitching. I froze out on the mound in Saturday's game, and the tension showed in my pitches. It almost cost us the game. I need you to help me all week before the championship game. Starting tonight," she added.

Connor chuckled. "Slow down. I promise to help but let me get settled, and then we can talk about the upcoming game and strategize." He knew they both had to be disappointed in his failure, but they sure didn't seem that way.

The hardest part would be telling his son. Added to that, telling Trey he had feelings for Lynette wouldn't go over well either. "Where's Trey?" he asked, ready to get this over with.

"Inside playing video games when he should be practicing, if you ask me," Gabby said, her voice filled with frustration.

"Thanks. I need to talk to him." It was easier to ignore her comment about practicing than to discuss his son's motivation, or lack thereof, to practice every free minute he had. Gabby had a fire inside that wouldn't be denied. Connor's job was to figure out what drove his son, and whatever it was, he would be supportive.

He went inside and was immediately greeted by Bingo. "Hey, boy. How are you?" he asked while rough housing with the dog a bit.

Woof. Woof. Bingo danced around with his tongue half hanging out and his tail wagging like a windshield wiper on high.

"Good boy," Connor said. Heading down the hall, he found Trey, glued to the game controller and playing a video game with total concentration. Enough he hadn't seen or heard Connor enter the room. "I'm back," Connor said loud enough for his son to hear.

After a quick glance up, Trey returned his focus to the screen, but not before Connor had seen the beginnings of a scowl. *You missed the most impor- tant game of his life. What did you expect?* The question buzzed in his head, reminding him of his failure at tryouts and with his son.

Something that was about to change.

"Can you turn that off? We need to talk." Connor stepped in front of Trey, blocking his view of the screen.

"Doesn't look like I have a choice." He tossed the controller on the sofa next to him.

It was a start, and Connor was the one who needed to close the communication gap between them. "Congratulations on the win. I was listening and heard it all play out. I'm proud of you, son."

"Whatever." Trey shrugged. "You weren't there. Mom wasn't there. No one cares what I do, so let's not pretend. Other than Principal Taylor and Keith, that is."

Connor flinched. There was so much hurt in Trey's voice, but it was the last part that sent him reeling. *Since when did his son and Lynette see eye to eye?* "That's not true, and you know it. I do care, and I wish things hadn't worked out the way they did. I wanted to be here, believe me. I only wanted what was best for us."

"Us? You trying out was all about you," Trey said, his expression one of disdain. "When does it end? And what am I supposed to do if you make it? Live with Keith? I might as well move in for all the time I'm here."

Connor ran his hands through his hair, trying to sort out his son's emotions. Trey might not ever forgive him, but it was his job to try and make it up to him. "That won't be an issue now. I didn't make the cut, so I'm home now—for good. Looks like you're stuck with me."

Trey looked up at him. "Looks like I need to accept second place in your life and be happy with it." His son sounded like Lynette.

They weren't second in his life. Okay, so maybe they had been, but they weren't anymore. Didn't that count for something? "It's not that way. Being the best of the best at something was as much to prove it to myself as it was to prove it to you. I wanted you to be proud of me, son." Connor was doing his best to gain Trey's understanding of the situation.

"Then it shouldn't be hard for you to understand I wanted you to be proud of me—but you weren't there." Trey wasn't giving an inch. The hurt that was reflected in his words ran deep—deeper than Connor had known or realized.

"I am proud. And I'll be here for the championship game. I'm sure you'll do just as well. It gives you another chance to show me what you got," Connor added, trying for a lighter note. Some common ground they could share to start over.

Trey shrugged. "I guess."

"Any chance you want to go out and grab some dinner at O'Malley's to celebrate your big win?" It was an olive branch tied to the one thing his son loved most—food.

"Sure. I'll be right there when I finish this game." His son's lack of exuberance wasn't what he'd hoped for, but at least Trey was giving him a chance. Everything he'd done had been for his son, and the best thing he could do now was to show his support.

This wasn't the right time to drop the Lynette bomb, but it had to be done. "One other thing. Any objection to me asking Lynette and Gabby to join us for dinner and the celebration? Gabby was a part of the win and it makes it more of a party."

Trey looked up in surprise and suddenly nodded. "Works for me," he said before returning his focus to the game.

Connor was stunned. Zero resistance and calm acceptance. What happened in the three days he was gone he couldn't begin to fathom, but he was anxious to find out. Coming home and staying home was the right decision.

It's not like you had a choice. They all kept saying he had made them his second choice, and the problem was, *they were right.*

Chapter Fourteen

♥

LYNETTE KNEW SHE AND Connor would face an uphill battle with the work issue looming between them, but there was no way she wanted to say no to his offer. And not just the offer for an evening of dinner and fun, but to them—as a couple. There would be a lot of concessions to be made once the board got wind of it, which in Hallbrook terms, meant faster than a baseball pitch to home plate.

Gabby was eager to go out to dinner at O'Malley's, surprising Lynette. She knew her daughter was growing close to Connor, but her *ewww* comments about the kiss she first witnessed seemed to have vanished.

Now, her daughter's disposition could only be termed as accepting, even encouraging. A change of heart if Gabby's help in picking out a pair of tan slacks and a light blue blouse was anything to go by. The color accented Lynette's eyes, which is why she'd bought it in the first place. It was one of the few indulgences she'd splurged on during the months of coming to grip with Dirk's passing, the color refreshing and spring-like.

The knock on the front door set her heart to racing. Her brother thought they were perfect for each other, and yet, they'd never even been on a date. Not alone anyway. She didn't think they could count the times at the pizza parlor surrounded by fifteen ballplayers.

"Mom, they're here. Let's go." Lynette looked down at her outfit and frowned. She would have preferred a pretty skirt and a blouse, but Connor had said a night of fun and to dress casually, so slacks would have to do.

"I'm coming." She walked down the hall into the living room, her pulse shooting up a few more notches when she took stock of Connor dressed in jeans and a sporty polo shirt that showed off his biceps and athletic body. His thick hair and olive complexion tanned from the sun were compliment-ed by the red fabric.

"You look nice. A little overdressed for casual in my world and for what we had in mind." Connor chuckled.

Not exactly what she was aiming for when she spent an hour getting ready. "*Ummm*, thanks, I think. I can change," she offered, unsure how to take his comment.

Connor shrugged. "You'll be fine if you don't mind getting your slacks or blouse a little dusty or dirty." He had the audacity to wink.

"Good grief. That would have been good need-to-know information. I'll change. So, *where* are we going?" She wasn't taking any chances the second time around.

"To the fields, of course." Connor grinned, his boyish charm shining through. She'd forgive him anything if he smiled at her like that all the time.

"Yes," Gabby exclaimed. "Does this mean you're going to help me with my pitching?"

"Some. But I thought you and Trey would enjoy some fun with baseball. Change up the pace to celebrate," Connor said.

"I like the sound of that," Trey chimed in.

"Give me a few minutes. I definitely need something else to wear if you expect me to help," Lynette said, turning to head back down the hall.

"Help? I don't think so." Connor's grin grew wider, the telltale deep dimples meaning he was up to something. "This time, you'll play. I'm thinking you should play outfield as I'm not sure you're up to catching Gabby's fastballs."

"Play? But I'm not very good. As in, I don't play at all," Lynette added.

"You don't have to be good. Everyone has to start somewhere. I'll put you in the outfield, and you can run after the balls and toss them back to Gabby to start with. Then we'll change things up. It's time you learned to pitch and hit like the kids. Join the fun. Be more than a team mom," he teased.

Look like a fool was more like it, but she didn't see any way to gracefully bow out. Otherwise, she'd look like a spoilsport. "Fine. Let me change clothes. And shoes," she added, glancing down at her heeled boots. Lynette wasn't all that coordinated and putting it out there for Connor and the kids to see wasn't high on her priority list.

It didn't take her long to find a pair of jeans and a T-shirt more suited to the activity she was being coerced into. Top that off with a not-so-new pair of sneakers, and she was ready to go. So much for dressing to impress.

They started out the door, Bingo trying to escape past them. He hated to be left behind, but with the evening they had planned, the dog wouldn't be a welcome fifth wheel. "Sorry, Bingo. You've got to stay here. I'll take you for a walk when we get back."

"He'll be fine, Mom. Come on," Gabby said.

"I'm coming." She patted the dog's side and gave him a final rub behind the ears, dropping a kiss on his head.

Twenty minutes later, they were at the fields. Lynette was relieved it looked as though no one else had the same idea. She rejoined the others and they headed for the ball field at the school.

Connor carried the duffel bag and led the way. "Trey, you bat first. Gabby, you pitch, and I'll catch," he said, taking control.

"Will do." Trey stepped up to the home plate.

Lynette headed for the outfield, out behind second base, hoping it would give her the easiest access to chase down the balls as they were drilled in her direction.

Trey swung the bat several times to warm up as Gabby pitched a few warm-up balls. Lynette, on the other hand, tried to find a way to make the oversized, awkward fitting glove open and close on her hand. She wasn't sure how anyone could catch a ball with it, especially not her. Athletics had never been her thing—something about a lack of eye-hand coordination.

As Gabby pitched to Trey, some were caught by Connor, others all too often, hit toward Lynette, or worse, past her. Chasing down the long drives hit into the outfield wasn't her idea of fun. And just as she suspected, the glove didn't work. Picking up the ball with her right hand was easier. It was also better to close the distance between her and Gabby before she threw. Otherwise, the ball always fell short, trickling toward her daughter like a kiddie throw.

The crack of the bat sounded, and the ball went high, straight in her direction. She held up her left hand, partly to protect herself and partly in hopes the ball wouldn't hit her. Call it self-defense.

Her heart pounded. Lynette desperately wanted to catch the ball just to show the others she could do it. The ball came at her as if in slow motion, hit the glove, and fell to the ground. Her face suffused with heat from embarrassment.

"Good try, Mom. Next time," Gabby called out, the grin on her face telling a different story.

"It's okay, Principal Taylor. It was a hard hit," Trey hollered as she threw the ball back to Gabby.

"You're doing great. Just keep your eye on the ball," Connor called out. "One more, and then we'll switch it up. I imagine Lynette's getting worn out while the rest of us are standing around."

Worn out was an understatement, but add to that a certain level of humiliation, she was more than ready to change places. Not that she'd be any better elsewhere. *What part of this was supposed to be fun?*

Gabby nodded and threw a pitch.

"Strike," Connor called out.

Trey shook his head. "One more. I want to end with a hit," he said, stepping back up to the plate.

"It may take you more than one then," Gabby teased.

"Hardy har-har." Trey grimaced, setting up to bat.

Connor said something to Trey but she was too far away to hear. The kid nodded. They were up to something—she could just feel it.

Gabby pitched the ball right down the middle.

Trey swung, the ball popping straight up and in her direction. *Again.*

Lynette got under the ball, keeping her eyes on it the way Connor instructed, and watching as the ball fell from the sky. She opened the glove wide, determined to get it right. The ball fell into her glove, and she covered it with her other hand, not willing to let it bounce off to the ground. Overjoyed, she held up the ball for all to see. "I got it. I got it," she called, running toward the others.

"Nice catch, Mom," Gabby said, giving her a high-five.

Trey nodded. "Good catch, Principal Taylor."

Connor came up, a huge grin on his face. "I knew you could do it."

"I kept thinking about what you said, and then it happened. It was amazing," she added, unable to contain her excitement. She handed the ball to Connor. "Can we do that again?"

"Watch out. She's hooked," Trey said.

Gabby nodded. "I think this time we should let the backstop catch the balls that go by me, and Coach can help Mom outfield. Trey can pitch."

Her daughter was up to no good judging by the gleam in her eyes. Clearly, Gabby had decided the idea of her and Connor together bode well for her pitching career. But was there more to it than that?

Trey handed off the bat to Gabby. "Sounds good to me. It's my turn to smoke a few pitches past *her*."

Gabby tilted her head to one side, her gaze on Trey. "And I like the sound of that," her daughter quipped.

Trey looked at her funny, as if unsure what she meant. "Of getting smoked by my pitches?" he asked, his brow furrowed. "That doesn't sound like you. Are you feeling okay?" he teased.

Her daughter grinned. "No, silly. You just admitted I smoked you with some of my pitches."

Chock one up for Gabby. Trey looked dumbfounded, but only for a second.

"Wow, I guess I did say that. And you did smoke the ball past me a few times." His comment surprised both her and Connor, judging by his surprised glance her way. A truce had been called between the two kids, something that would make her and Connor's decision to enter a relationship easier.

"I guess we can field together. It'll give you a break out here." Connor grinned, something he did quite often lately.

Trey managed to pitch some good balls, but Gabby managed to connect with several, sending her and Connor chasing the balls down all over the field.

"This is going to be a fastball. Call it a fair warning," Trey hollered.

Gabby adjusted her body position slightly and swung hard as the ball ripped toward her. The bat connected, and the ball flew high and long.

Lynette was the closest, and she took off running, determined to make another great catch. She kept her eye on the ball, glove in the air. *Just a little further now.* Her heart pounded in her chest, drowning out whatever Connor was yelling. She knew without him telling her that she needed to move back more. Turning to the right, she extended her arm and jumped as it started to sail over her head.

Ooommph. She collided with a hard mass of body. The ball hit her glove and fell to the ground, she and Connor toppling over one another.

It took her a second to catch her breath. "I could have had that ball if you hadn't interfered," she said, frowning over at him.

Connor shook his head. "Didn't you hear me calling the ball? That generally means you should back off."

Lynette couldn't believe he was saying it was her fault. "You ran into me. All I heard was back or something like that. So I turned back and reached for it."

Connor rolled to the side and stood, offering Lynette a hand and pulling her to her feet. He smiled at her. "Quite the opposite, as I was telling you to back off the ball. I'm glad to see you're not hurt."

"Hey, you two, I thought we were practicing, not necking," Trey hollered.

"You mean rubbernecking?" Gabby chimed in, and the two kids burst out laughing.

Lynette frowned as she dusted off her jeans. "It's not necking," she told them, trying to set the record straight. "I don't believe in public displays of affection."

"PDA, Mom. That's what it's called," Gabby said, her daughter and Trey headed their way. "Maybe we should go eat. I think mom has had enough. Not to mention, I'm hungry."

Trey grabbed his stomach with an exaggerated grip to his mid-section. "Don't know how you could want to eat. PDA between our parents is turning my stomach."

"You two are full of yourselves tonight. Let's grab our stuff and head for dinner. At least with food in your mouth, you can't talk." Leave it to Connor to join in the fray.

Lynette thought it better to stay out of the kid's line of fire and to second her daughter's emotion. "I concur, with the hungry part, that is."

Who knew baseball practice could be such a contact sport?

Or considered an opportunity for a PDA?

Chapter Fifteen

❤

THE PAST TWO NIGHTS were more of the same with Lynette and the kids. Connor had even added in movies, miniature golf, and a stop at the Peterson's Creamery for ice cream. All things that could be enjoyed by the four of them. They had clicked into place like a ready-made family.

Tonight, however, was just for him and Lynette. *Their first real date.*

He'd be lying if he didn't admit to the nerves that came with the event. Keith's support made it easier, knowing his best friend was all for them going out. But a small part of Connor hadn't quite jumped in with both feet, and it had nothing to do with Lynette. The woman was nothing short of amazing, and he enjoyed her laughter, teasing, and even the more serious side.

There had been several comments from other teachers, everyone acting as though they'd known something was going on all along, but so far, there were no real issues. And it wasn't as if he was looking for a promotion, or pushing for a higher athletic budget, or any of the number of things that could raise eyebrows with regards to special concessions. Not to mention, they avoided seeing each other at school at all costs to avoid any awkwardness.

Several times he'd wanted to stop by. Once, he even thought about sending flowers. A romantic side of himself he hadn't even known existed—and one that surprised him. He cared about Lynette in a way he didn't remember feeling for his first wife.

Young love was sometimes more of a rush to start life and not based on true connection. It took time to realize who you were and what you wanted out of life, and when two young people matured and discovered they were on opposite sides of the spectrum, the marriage failed. Much the same way he and Darlene self-destructed.

The past few days had shown Connor a side of life he hadn't expected to enjoy, but surprisingly, he did. The hole in his heart from the failure at tryouts was slowly closing, but he understood it would take a while to come to grips with the finality. Not that he'd share those feelings with anyone.

Sharply at seven, he headed next door and knocked. Lynette answered, stunning him with her beauty. "Wow," he said, finding his vocal cords seconds later. "You look fabulous." Total understatement. With a yellow form-fitted blouse and pink, yellow, and a loose blue skirt of soft material that hung gracefully, stopping at her thighs, she was the epitome of fresh beauty. Long legs that ended with spiked heels, bringing her close to his height. Not an easy task. Her chestnut hair had been freed from her usual principal bun, as he liked to call it. Instead, it hung loosely on her shoulders, framing her face. Large blue eyes gazed at him, her dark lashes highlighting the intensity of their color.

"Thank you. You look pretty good yourself." She grinned, taking the arm he offered.

His heart raced as he led her to the truck. "It's not the same. I've seen you in office mode with suits or slacks, casual jean mode, and even dressy casual, but dressed to the nines, that's another story." In fact, Connor felt slightly underdressed in slacks and a button-down shirt. At least he'd worn a tie. But then it didn't matter how he looked because all eyes would be on the gorgeous woman next to him.

"Thanks, I think." She laughed, leaning toward him and dropping a kiss on his cheek.

The next time she tried that move he vowed to be quicker and turn his head ever so slightly. A real kiss would have been far more rewarding. "I'll have to take you out more often on a date if this is what's in store."

"Sounds like a plan to me." After she slid in the passenger seat, he closed the door and made his way to the driver's side.

"Where are we going?" she asked.

"I thought we should head to Lancaster. One of the other teachers had mentioned a place the other day that sounded perfect for a private date. It's called Table Divine. I made us reservations for seven-thirty."

"It sounds lovely."

Lynette's fragrance wafted in his direction and Connor breathed in its essence. It wasn't strong, the delicate orange and rose scents fresh, like her. He reached for her hand, grateful the vehicle was an automatic. "Your scent is lovely," he said, using Lynette's choice of wording to cover his nerves.

"Interesting term for a...guy," she teased.

He enjoyed her smile, even when she was turning the tables on him. "You know what I mean. Your fragrance is summer fresh. Is that better?" he asked.

"A teeny bit and thank you. You're far too easy to tease."

He was blowing it. When the kids were around, his confidence level soared. But one on one, he was no good at this sort of thing. "Sorry. It must be my lack of experience dating."

"You? Mr. Baseball. I'm sure you have lots of women who hit on you, and that you had quick and ready compliments on your lips."

That's where she was wrong. He'd never fit into that scene—but then he'd had a wife and son at home. It had meant something to him, even if it hadn't for Darlene. "Guess again," he said dryly, not liking the implication.

Lynette pulled back, half turning in her seat to face him. "Well, then. We have something else in common. I have the same lack of experience, so relax. We'll muddle through this together."

"Sounds like a plan," he said, grateful for the pass on his dating skills.

It didn't take long before he was parking the truck, and they were seated at an alcove toward the back of Table Divine. It was everything his friend has said and more. Romance was in the air, jazz music playing softly.

They sat next to each other on one side of the semi-round booth. Connor took her hand, feeling as though it would help calm his nerves. It was as if he were sixteen again and on his first date. But they'd already shared one strawberry kiss, and Connor was looking forward to another.

"So what do you think of the new camaraderie between the kids? I still find it baffling, but I'm not arguing." Lynette took a sip of wine, gazing at him. Her eyes almost looked black, with her pupils dilated in the low light.

Connor shrugged. "I have no idea. I thought I would have a difficult time with Trey when I told him we were going to date, but the reaction I got was quite the opposite. It's almost as if they have secretly put a stamp of approval on us being together." He let his thumb caress the back of her hand.

"I agree. But I need to tell you something you should know. I'm concerned that Gabby is looking at you as far more than a coach. I've wondered if she's not using you to replace her father. How do you feel about that, knowing it in advance? I mean, I don't want us to do anything for the kids, but we do have to be careful we don't do anything to hurt them in the process."

It was something Connor had thought about earlier but discarded. He had no more control over the kid's reactions than he had of his own future. "I hadn't considered that with regards to Gabby. She's a great kid, and I enjoy working with her. She's very coachable. As to the rest, let's just wait and see how it all plays out and deal with issues when they arise. We agreed to dating, but there's no pressure for this to go anywhere. *One day at a time* is my motto."

Lynette let out a deep breath and nodded. "Okay then. One day at a time." She raised her glass for a toast, and Connor obliged, raising his own and clinking them together.

The only problem was that Connor wasn't convinced Lynette meant the words.

Lynette may have agreed to Connor's suggestion to take things one day at a time, but it wasn't in her nature to live that way. At least, not anymore. Living that way in the past had taught her the folly in that line of thinking. The kids would be hurt if things didn't work out between them. For that matter, Lynette didn't want to be hurt either.

Connor was in town to stay, so there was that. And he was a great guy. And from the beginning, she'd known she cared about him more than she should have. Maybe she should simply trust him and trust the feelings that had been rekindled in her heart. *Loving someone.*

Scary—but nice. More than nice. Comfortable and exciting all rolled into one. "I'm glad we finally got a chance to do this. You know, go out without the kids. We came here to Lancaster to avoid the gossips, but I'm not sure that's working. Next time, we should just go to O'Malley's. It's not as if everyone hasn't already seen the four of us together all over town," Lynette said, letting some of her thoughts become vocalized. Others, she'd keep a close watch on.

Connor nodded. "I agree about the gossips. I hear comments every day at school, and even before we agreed to do this, people had us in a relationship." He reached for her hand. "I do like the idea that after tonight you want to go out with me again. I must be doing something right." He winked as he gave her one of those charming smiles that made her toes curl.

"Mr. Thomas approached me today about us, and I told him the truth. I also told him what we discussed about stepping out of the way should there be a conflict of interest on any voting processes. He seemed okay with everything, so maybe we were overthinking it."

"As president of the school board, his opinion would carry a lot of weight. I'm glad we have him on our side." Connor's thumb caressed the back of her hand. "Heck, add to that we have the kids on our side, and how can we lose?" He chuckled.

"True." Lynette knew he was right, but the tiny seed of doubt wouldn't let go. She shoved it aside, determined not to let the seed sprout, and determined to enjoy the evening.

"I've been meaning to ask you something," Connor said, his voice serious but with a lack of the normal confidence she'd come to expect from him.

"Ask away."

"I know this is still a couple of weeks off, and I know it's not your favorite thing to do, but I'm hoping you'll agree to it. For me."

"Quit beating around the bush and ask. What's the worst I can do? Say no," she teased. He acted as though he was asking a girl to prom and afraid of rejection. Something Lynette was certain would have never happened back then...or now.

"Well, you see, reservations have to be made a year in advance to get the best site, and I was wondering if you'd consider going camping with us? Trey and me, that is. And, of course, Gabby."

Camping. Not what she expected—or wanted to repeat. A year was a long time away. Long enough to change her mind. And long enough to see where she stood with Connor. "Sure. Book away, I'll pencil it my calendar for next summer." Pencil because it was easy to erase. Just the thought of the snakes gave her the shivers.

"Not next year. In two weeks. Father's Day weekend. When I came home after the injury, I booked one of the best sites the day the reservation window opened for those dates. Trey's been looking forward to it all year. I think it would be fun to have you and Gabby join us."

"Trey might not agree. He really wants some alone father-son time with you." Code for *I don't want to go.*

"He'll be happy we're still going. When I left for tryouts, he was pretty upset with me, partly because of the importance of his games coming up, but also because he thought I was ditching him for Father's Day."

"I don't know." Lynette wasn't sure how to back out of this hole she'd created for herself. There wasn't a single logical explanation she could come up with for why she'd go in a year and not now. Illogical for her was snakes and bugs.

"Come on, say yes. The kids will have a blast. Last time you weren't prepared, and it wasn't much fun—this time I'll help you decide what to pack.

Besides, the site is amazing, and even if you just sit on the shore admiring the view, it'll be worth it. I promise." His smile made everything hard to resist.

Boyish charm. Lynette swallowed hard. "Okay. Gabby will love it, I'm sure," she forced the words from her lips before she could change her mind.

"This time around, you will too. I'll even pack the Snake-Away." He chuckled.

"You're kidding, right? Is there such a thing?"

Connor nodded, his grin growing wider. "Yes, there is, but I am kidding. Stuff is useless out in the woods. The snakes truly don't want anything to do with you."

"I'll take your word for it because I don't want to ask them in person." Her sense of humor returned. Probably because she was lost in Connor's warm brown eyes, and it had addled her brain.

The evening flew past all too quickly, and after lingering over a shared crème brûlée, they headed home. The drive was peaceful, small talk on the after-dinner menu. They discussed school, and the end of the year, and even some things they could do together with the kids. Mostly about the camping trip she'd agreed to.

What was she thinking?

They pulled into the driveway and got out of the truck. Connor took her arm and led her next door, stopping on the front porch. He pulled her close. "I've been waiting for this all evening," he murmured.

"Saying good night? Was our date that awful?" she asked, a teasing grin on her face.

"Not at all. But there was something missing from tonight's dessert." He lowered his head toward her, mere inches separating them.

Her heart raced as she tried to focus on his words and his lips. "What was missing? I thought it was fabulous."

"Strawberry," he said, his voice husky with emotion just as he captured her mouth against his.

There was no need to ask what he meant. She gave herself over to his tender kiss, vowing that come tomorrow, she'd stock up on her favorite lip gloss. *Apparently, it was Connor's favorite also.*

Chapter Sixteen

♥

IT WAS GETTING INCREASINGLY difficult to keep the attention of the kids in PE. The end of the school year was near, and summer vacation plans were the center of every discussion. The day wore on as he tried to keep the students focused on giving it their all as they played outdoor games designed for fun and exercise.

By three, he was more than ready to go home. He logged off the computer after inputting the student's attendance records. Connor's phone vibrated against the wood of his desk. It wasn't a number he recognized, and he almost killed the call to mark it as spam.

Instead, he grabbed his briefcase and headed for the door, pressing the green button to accept the call. "Connor Weston," he said, ready to hang up at the first sign it was a sales call.

"Connor, glad I was able to reach you. This is Herbert Farnsworth, from the Southside Red Sox minor league administration office."

He didn't recognize the name, but at the mention of the Red Sox minor leagues, he stopped walking. Adrenaline shot through him, his heart racing. Could this be the call? Maybe there had been a mistake. He couldn't control his reaction any more than he could control the wind. It had been a part of him for so long, even if he had recently vowed it was all behind him.

"I was just on my way home. What's up?" He tried to place the man's name but came up short.

"I work for Mr. Masters, the owner of the team. After some discussion over the past couple of days, we'd like to offer you a place within the organization. We think you would be an asset and are prepared to offer you a lucrative package."

"Seriously?" Connor's hand shook. Thirty years old and acting like a rookie. This was a dream come true, or at least one in the making. "Let me get this straight. You need a backup pitcher or something, and you want me for the position? I swear you won't regret this." He couldn't keep the exhilaration out of his voice, the rush of adrenaline hitting him hard.

"No, no. Slow down, Connor. You and I both know these younger kids are coming up through the ranks more developed and confident. Most have been playing since they learned to walk."

The word *no* was like a knife to the gut. The double no solidified he'd heard the man correctly. Connor was used to rejection, but this time, he hadn't been prepared for it. "Then what?" he asked, fighting back against the empty feeling.

"You talked to Alvin Smith at tryouts and gave him some tips on a couple of the players," Herbert offered, as though it were a full explanation.

"Yeah. So what? It wasn't anything they didn't know." Connor remembered watching the players. It was when he knew the truth about his chances of making it on the team were nonexistent. He just hadn't been able to let go until he saw his name on the cut list.

"Actually, that's not true. The coach talked to us. Because of what you said he picked one of the kids to pitch for us—someone Alvin almost overlooked. You have a deep understanding of what a player needs and can look beneath the surface stats. For that reason, we want to offer you a coaching and scouting position with the team. We're hoping you'll work with this kid and a few other players, getting them fine-tuned and mentally ready for what's ahead of them. Like I said before, we think you'd be a great asset to the league."

Connor let out a deep breath. They wanted him—as a coach. It wasn't anything he'd ever considered before. The idea started as a seed, quickly blossoming into reality—and more than a little exciting.

If he started with the minors and proved himself, there was an excellent chance that in time, he'd move to coach in the majors. His dream might have been to play, but the opportunity to coach was equally amazing. "I'm interested. Tell me more," he said. *Yes. Yes. Yes.* That's what he really wanted to say, but he needed the particulars.

He would be joining the team and going on the road with them. Connor did a fist pump as he processed the details. The salary was golden. More than he'd earned even playing in the minors.

"What do you think?" Herbert asked when he finished laying out the package.

There was only one answer Connor could give. "I'm in. When do I start?"

"That's the one catch-22 to all this. We need you to drive down here tomorrow morning. The bus leaves for Chicago at two, and we want you on it. You can work with some of the kids on the mental aspects of the game and get a feel for their abilities before Saturday's game."

Saturday's game. The words clicked in his head, reminding him of another game on Saturday. *The championship game.* He closed his eyes and rubbed his forehead, tension clouding his earlier excitement. Trey would be devastated.

"Is there any way I can start the following week? My son's championship game is this weekend and I promised him I'd be there." He had to try and do what was right for his son.

"I understand, I do. Unfortunately, you know how this all works. This kid has a million-dollar arm, and we need it in action. The team can't take any more losses this year, and we invested heavily in the boy. Time is money, and you know it as well as I do.

It's a great opportunity. The next stop would be the majors if you prove yourself as a good handler for these young showoffs. Gotta pay to play," Herbert added.

Something Connor knew all too well. But still, it was Trey's game. He closed his eyes, not wanting to make a final decision. *Except he had to.* His whole life had led him to this moment, and there was only one choice he could make. In the long run, it would be better for Trey, even if his son didn't understand it now. "I'll be there." This was his future, and he'd been handed a silver lining in all the disappointment he'd faced.

"Great. I'll see you tomorrow." Herbert hung up, leaving Connor staring at the phone.

This was happening fast, and there was no time to prepare Trey for the inevitable. They'd have to talk about what it meant if Connor was on the road. In the best-case scenario, Trey could hit the road with him.

Except for this weekend. Trey needed to be here—for his team. And for himself. Connor wouldn't take that away from his son. Doubts settled in, the euphoria he felt at being hired on as a coach dissipating quickly.

His son would never forgive him if he missed the championship game. Neither would Gabby. And then there was Lynette.

Lynette would be angry and hurt at his decision, and rightly so. This opportunity was a miracle, and Lynette's stance on the subject left him no choice but to end things between them. She'd never understand his decision to leave, and she'd left him in no doubt of her opinion on the stability factor in her life. Something he could no longer promise her. He would never ask Lynette to give up her dreams, any more than she should ask him to do the same.

At one point, he'd thought professional baseball was a thing of the past and his hopes and dreams were locked up tight in a never-to-be-opened box, but the sudden euphoria he'd felt at the offer was a sure sign the box had never truly been locked.

He could only hope Trey would forgive him for what he was about to do. There wasn't much time to get everything ready. Boston was a two-and-a-half-hour drive, and he'd have to leave early in the morning. Lynette would need time to find a temporary fill-in for his PE classes, but at least the school year was almost over.

Connor pulled into the driveway. Letting out a deep sigh, he knew he needed to get the next part over with. *Telling everyone.* "Trey, I'm home. You here?" he called out from the living room, tossing his briefcase on the sofa.

"In the kitchen." His son came through the doorway holding a sandwich. "What's up?"

"I need to talk to you about something."

Trey grinned, plopping himself down on the sofa. "Sure. You can talk, and I'll eat," he said, taking a huge bite.

His son's appetite never ceased to amaze him. "Something has come up that changes things for us. I'm hoping you'll be just as excited about it as I am." In truth, he expected no such thing, but it didn't hurt to pave the way with hope.

"Why don't I like the sound of this already?" Trey asked, taking another bite of his sandwich, his brow furrowed.

"It's all in how you look at it, son. I've been offered a coaching opportunity with the Southside Red Sox minor league team. They want me to work with the new guys that are still wet behind the ears, so to speak. I'll help fine-tune their pitches, fielding abilities, and work on their life skills and how to deal with living on the road. Like a coach and mentor, all rolled into one. *And* they want me as a scout for new talent."

His son looked at him in disbelief, a scowl forming on his face. "What changes are you talking about? I like it right where we are."

So much for holding out hope—Trey's attitude already on the defensive. "I need to be on the road with the team and you could come with me and homeschool. You'd have a blast and get to learn so much from the upstarts rising through the ranks. Not to mention the exposure and connections you'd make for your own future with baseball." Connor was doing his best to paint a rosy picture.

Trey stood, shaking his head. "Sounds like you have it all worked out. But none of this takes into consideration what I want. When does what I want start mattering to you? It doesn't matter to Mom, and now, you expect me to drop everything and go with you. I don't want to. And if you'd bother to ask me first, you'd know that." His son tossed his napkin into the trash can, and slammed the cupboard door shut.

He hated the idea of letting Trey down, but he hated not being a positive role model for his son even more. "This is good for both of us. Why can't you see that?"

"Why can't you see it from my point of view? I'm tired of all the changes. I just want to be a regular kid. Not some famous guy's son who's never around. Is that so hard to understand?"

Connor jerked back, reeling from not only his son's comment but the anger in which it was delivered. None of which changed anything but left him with a deep ache in his heart for what had to be done. "I'm sorry you feel that way. I've already accepted and it's the right thing to do for you and me as a family."

"I'm not going. That's your thing, so leave. I'll stay with Keith," Trey fumed.

Connor had expected this conversation might not go well, but nothing could have prepared him for the intensity of Trey's response. "I'm not sure he—"

"Talk to him. I'm not going. My friends are here. Summer vacation is here. I want to spend my days relaxing with friends, swimming at the lake, and camping. I want a chance to be a kid, not a piece of baggage you haul around because you have to."

Ouch. It was pointless to argue, especially given his son had a point—to a certain degree. For now, at least, he knew Keith would let him stay next door. There was only another week of school. "I'll talk to him. And for what it's worth, I'm sorry this is the way it has to be. It's an excellent opportunity, and I'd be a fool to pass it up."

"That's the problem. It's always been your way." Trey huffed. "When are you leaving?"

"Tomorrow morning." Connor felt awful as the words slipped out of his mouth. Trey's rejection chipped away at more of the joy he'd felt when he accepted the offer.

"I'm out of here. Do what you want, but don't include me in your plans." His son stormed out of the room without so much as a backward glance, the front door slamming shut seconds later.

And Connor wasn't so sure his next meeting would go any better. He stood, took a deep breath, and headed next door. Might as well get the inevitable over with. He still needed to pack, but he wouldn't shirk his responsibility in telling Lynette his decision face to face. He knocked on the door and waited. Gabby answered, stepping back to let him in. Bingo moved in for an exciting hello of his own.

"What's up, Coach?" she asked, stepping back to let him inside.

"I need to talk with your mother. Is she here?" he asked, patting the dog and trying to settle him down.

"Hang on. You two are like inseparable. Geesshh." She grinned, heading toward the hallway. "Mom, your boyfriend is here to see you," she called out in a sing-song voice.

Boyfriend. One word that held a wealth of meaning and one that would cease to exist by the time he left. It was the right thing to do, but it didn't make it any easier.

"Hey there," Lynette said, coming into the room. "I wasn't expecting you this early. Or did I get the time wrong for our date tonight?"

Connor shook his head, knowing the time was at hand. "Some things have come up, and I can't make it tonight. I'm sorry for the last-minute notice." And for everything else he had to tell her.

"Oh, is everything all right?" she asked, her brow creasing with concern.

"Yes. No. Can we talk? Outside perhaps," he added, not wanting Gabby to overhear what he had to say.

"*Ummm*...sure," Lynette said, turning to head for the back door, leaving him to follow.

"What's up, Connor? You seem as though something is wrong. It's making me nervous."

He took her by the hand and drew her close. "Things are right and wrong. It's a mixed bag of emotions for sure, but the thing of it is, I got a call earlier that changes things for me. I've been offered a coaching job with the Southside Red Sox minor league team." He went on to explain it to her, much like he'd done with Trey and with the same results. *Disbelief. Disappointment. Denial.*

She pulled away from him. "So you're leaving? When?" Lynette asked, her voice crisp with tension.

But it was the tears that glistened in her eyes that twisted his stomach in knots.

"Tomorrow. I'm sorry it's such short notice, but they've got a game this weekend in Chicago. I'll be traveling with the team on a regular basis. I'm still trying to work out the details with Trey. He's not overly receptive to the idea."

She folded her arms in front of her chest as if in self-defense. "Neither am I. I won't follow you around the country, and I won't be sitting at home waiting on your return. I won't give up myself again," Lynette said, the firm resolve in her voice crystal clear.

It was nothing short of what he expected her to say. At least they found out this was happening before they'd gotten more involved as a couple, or a family. More than anything, he wanted her to understand. "I'm not asking you to. I know it wouldn't be fair. But I can't give up on my dreams either. They changed slightly, but it's still the same. And I can't be a PE teacher and a coaching dad when I know there's more than that for my life. My future. Baseball is my life."

Lynette's mouth hung open and then closed. Opened and closed again. "So, just like that, you decide. Whatever was between us is already over without so much as a discussion. It must be nice to run your life with such an iron grip, not considering anyone else but yourself. Not even Trey."

"I'm sorry. It's better this way, and you know it. I care alot about you, maybe more than that, but I also know you crave stability—something I can't give you. As for Trey, he needs the action. This is a chance to show him what it takes to dream big. I failed to get into the majors as a player, but here's my shot to show him his old man can be successful in a different way."

She shook her head and took a few steps back as if putting distance between them would help. "I should have known better than to give in and try to have a relationship with you. I'd always be second best to baseball, and that's not a competition I care to compete in. I should have never let my guard down."

"I'm sorry." There wasn't much else he could say, and he knew it. Talking wouldn't change anything.

"Sorry doesn't make the hurt fade any faster. Just go. Keith and I will take care of the team and the championship game Saturday. *We* won't let them down. Although, I'm not sure how this will go over. Last time they won for you. I'm not so sure they'll be as forgiving this go round."

"They need to do their best for themselves, not me. That's what this is all about. Doing your best and living with the consequences, win or lose. It's the same thing I'm doing, living with the consequences. But I have to take my shot at something bigger and better."

"I hope you're happy, Connor. Truly, I wish you the best." Tears trickled down Lynette's face, and she furiously brushed them aside. "Goodbye."

Watching her walk away was worse than his heart breaking, it was as if his heart were being ripped out of his chest. "Goodbye, Lynette," he said, even though she couldn't hear him.

Connor was sure he'd half fallen in love with Lynette, which made it all the more difficult to leave. But it couldn't change the outcome—he had to take the job.

For himself.

Anything less would leave him empty inside.

Chapter Seventeen

♥

"**I** STILL DON'T SEE why Coach had to leave. Doesn't he care about the team?" Gabby asked on the way to school Friday morning.

Lynette paused, trying to find the right words. "Honey, he does. This is called life. Sometimes, we have to make tough choices. I'm sure Connor would have liked to stick around, but he got a great job offer. It's not the kind that comes around often, and he'd have missed his chance to become part of something even bigger. His whole life is baseball. I'm sure you can see and understand that." It sounded like perfectly good reasoning as she echoed Connor's words. Unfortunately, her heart wasn't listening.

"I guess. It stinks he couldn't be here for the game," Gabby said, turning to look out the window.

Her daughter wasn't buying the logic any more than Lynette was. If only she hadn't let her heart get involved. "I agree, but also know it doesn't change the reason for the game. The team worked hard to make it to the championship game, and now they simply need to go in there and do their best. Your Uncle Keith and I will do what we can to coach, and everyone on the team will need to give one hundred and ten percent of effort. It's all we can do." *Given the circumstances.* That part Lynette kept to herself. She'd also kept the break up from reaching her daughter's ears. There was plenty of time to tell her, and Lynette was holding off the disappointment and anger Gabby was sure to experience.

"Trey was pretty upset when I talked to him last night," Gabby said as she grabbed her backpack.

"I'm sure. It's a lot more involved for him because of the impact on his life. Just continue to be his friend. Which, by the way, since when did you two become chummy?"

Gabby shrugged. "I don't know. Hanging out a lot, I guess. I liked the way he stood up for me against Riley. Hard to hold a grudge against him after that, no matter what dumb-boy things he does." Gabby grinned.

"Have a good day at school, honey," she said, dropping her off at the front entrance.

"Bye, Mom." Gabby waved, hopping out of the car. They had to keep the line moving to get everyone to class on time.

Lynette parked in the teacher's area and entered the building through the side door. She poured a fresh cup of coffee in the teacher's lounge and headed for her office. Gabby's questions brought home some of Lynette's own issues with what happened with Connor. Everything she'd told her daughter was true, but the problem was, deep down, she knew she'd failed her friendship with Connor. She hadn't supported him or been happy about the job offer. In fact, she'd turned her back on him—not that he'd asked her to stick around.

But then, did he say what he said, knowing Lynette had been adamant she wasn't interested in a chaotic relationship? It was the one common denominator she'd made clear when agreeing to a relationship in the first place. The only two things she hadn't counted on were him leaving and her falling in love. Or at least that's what it felt like, contrary to what she'd admitted to him. The ache in the region of her heart wasn't a medical problem—it was an emotional one.

Each day she looked forward to seeing him, whether in passing at school or after school. And knowing he was headed to Boston this morning and then on to Chicago meant he'd be gone for days. She would miss seeing him all the time.

Was she wrong to end things with Connor? It wasn't a life she wanted anymore or hadn't planned on. But she also hadn't planned on caring for him as much as she did. Love wasn't something you could control, but life was.

Compromise.

The word came out of nowhere and settled in her stomach like a Christmas fruitcake. Heavy, unfulfilling, and stuck to the roof of her mouth. A compromise would require traveling, something her job wouldn't allow. Or Connor could travel, and she could stay put—like she'd done with Dirk.

That hadn't worked out so well.

Off-season wouldn't be so bad, and it's not like he'd be gone nine months to a year at a time.

Lynette played out the scenarios, both the pros and cons. Her training as a military wife had taught her how to manage a chaotic life.

She shoved aside her wayward thoughts, knowing it was a fruitless waste of time. They had both made their choices, and Connor was gone. Lynette refused to come second in his life like she had with Dirk. She wanted family to come first—something other military families managed quite well. It was Dirk who signed up every chance he got to be deployed or move to a new base, thirsting for excitement and change. Never once had he bothered to consult her, and therein lay the problem.

Connor hadn't consulted her either. He simply made the decision and left.

Lynette busied herself with checking over student progress reports. By lunch, she was ready to make a clean exit and get some fresh air. Grabbing her purse, she headed for the door.

Mary Ellen was hard at work, the secretary looking up as Lynette approached. "I'm going to lunch. I should be back in about forty-five minutes."

"No problem, boss. I'll hold down the fort until then."

Mary Ellen would have a stack of messages waiting for her return, but until then, Lynette was free. She'd packed her lunch this morning, finding it costly to run to the diner every day. And eating at the cafeteria wasn't high on her priority list. Not that the food was bad, more because she valued the escape from the confines of the school for a midday refresh.

Lynette let the door close behind her, turning left to leave, and almost running into one of the students. "I'm so sorry," she said, jerking her lunch bag over her head to keep it from getting squished between them.

"Sorry, Principal Taylor," Trey said, suddenly looking like he wanted to be anywhere except standing in the hallway talking to her.

"Totally my fault." She grinned. "What's up? Shouldn't you be at the cafeteria? I heard it's spaghetti day."

"I'm not hungry. And err, *umm*, I wanted to talk to you." He shoved his hands in his pockets and scuffed his feet on the floor—a telltale sign something was wrong.

Lynette's heart went out to the kid. He had a lot to deal with, and if she could help, she would. "I was just heading outside to eat. Want to join me?"

Trey shrugged. "I guess." His downcast expression spoke volumes.

"Hold on. Let me tell Mrs. Walters what we're doing." She poked her head back in the office. "Trey Weston is going to take a walk with me. If anyone calls looking for him, let them know. We should be back soon, and definitely before his next class."

"Will do, boss." Mary Ellen jotted down the information and nodded.

"Let's go," Lynette said, falling in next to Trey as they headed for the exit door. After leaving the building, she turned to him. "Let's head for the bleachers. It's a good place to talk and eat lunch. So, what's on your mind?" She had a good idea but needed to hear it from him first.

"It's my dad and his new job." Trey's voice had dropped low, and she strained to capture the words.

"I figured as much. How do you feel about it?" she asked, using the questions as an opportunity to let him unload the pent-up emotions he was experiencing.

"I reckon it doesn't matter how I feel. It never has. But...it's just I wish it did. I want to stay in Hallbrook. Stay with the team. Keep my friends. He's talking about making me homeschool on the road. Don't I have any say-so in this?" Trey's passionate response caught her off guard. The first part was understandable, but his desire to stay in town came as a surprise. Connor would be heartbroken to know where his son's line of thinking had fallen, and that Trey was actively seeking information on how to avoid his father's decree.

"The fact is, in your situation, your dad has the final say so. Twelve isn't old enough to make those kinds of decisions for yourself, but I think you need to talk to your dad. Let him know how you feel." She wasn't about to give him anything for ammo in a case against his father. It was better to help him reach for a discussion phase, something it would seem was long overdue between the two.

"I have. He's not listening. It's always that he wants to make me proud. Wants us to be happy. I think it's about him being happy and not us." Trey's sullen expression had only intensified on the walk to the bleachers.

They sat down, Lynette scrambling for what to say to him. "Your dad has worked hard for this, and it's a special opportunity. I totally understand both sides of the situation. I prefer the stability now, having led a chaotic life prior to this. But your dad and I are two different people, and he's your father. He loves you." That was the most important thing Trey needed to hear—*every child did.*

"He has a funny way of showing it," Trey mumbled.

Lynette wanted to hug him but knew that would be crossing boundaries at school. At home tonight, she'd be sure to pay him extra attention. "Try talking to him again. Calmly. It sounds as though nothing has been decided yet with regards to your future, so there's still hope this will all work out."

"I wish Keith would adopt me. Then I could stay here with you and him." Trey's words shocked Lynette.

His anger was much deeper than the surface, and he'd been hurt by the divorce more than anyone knew. The boy wanted stability as much as Lynette did, albeit for different reasons. "My brother loves having you around, as do I. Tell you what, why don't we focus on the championship game tomorrow, and then we can focus on what happens next when your dad returns. There's no sense in borrowing trouble that's not here yet. Make sense?" Summer vacation started soon and it would allow for a lot of options with regards to Trey.

"I guess. He missed my last game. I'm still mad about that, but I'm glad you were there. And Keith. At least someone who cares saw it."

Trey was still smarting over his father's absence, making this new twist all that much harder to understand. Tomorrow was the championship game, and all this kid wanted was for his father to be there. Except, Connor had made his decision and it didn't include the Legal Eagles or tomorrow's game.

"Keith and I care very much, and we were proud of you. Your dad is too. Trust me. I'll let you in on a little secret. I know your father recorded the footage of your winning hit from the school's video onto his phone. And I've caught him watching it a time or two since then." It was something she should have tried to understand better. Connor was making choices he didn't necessarily agree with, but he made them because he didn't feel he had a choice. He loved his son, but he needed to consider their future.

"Really?" Trey asked, his eyes widening in interest.

Lynette nodded. The kid had to be hungry, seeing as he hadn't eaten breakfast this morning before catching the bus. He could have ridden in with her, but he preferred seeing his friends. "Really. Here, eat half my peanut butter and jelly sandwich. And have a cookie. It'll make me feel better if you've eaten something." She held out her hand, waiting for him to snatch it up.

"Strawberry jelly?" he asked.

"Of course. What else is there for a PB&J?"

"Nothing." Trey grinned, taking the sandwich from her. "Thanks," he said, stuffing it into his mouth for a big bite.

Trey was a bit angry and confused, but at least he felt comfortable talking to her about the issues. All kids needed to feel as though someone was listening, and the two of them had come a long way since they'd first met. But then, so had Connor and Gabby. Lynette still hadn't told her daughter about the breakup, even though she'd had several opportunities.

After the game would be better.

Mile after mile, the bus rolled down the highway as it headed for Chicago. Three hours into the trip and Connor started having second thoughts. Technically, his thinking time included the drive to Boston.

The lure and excitement kept the doubts at bay, but now, here on the bus, the image of his son's face when he went next door to say goodbye came back to him. Trey wasn't a happy camper, not by any stretch of the imagination. It wasn't that Connor didn't understand the kid's reasons, but his son wasn't considering any of this from Connor's perspective. *Their future.*

The die was cast, and Connor had made his decision. It was a life-long dream, slightly modified, but something that put him in the same big picture. Major league baseball. The call of the crowd, the rush of success. Moments and memories that would last a lifetime.

Trey would get over his disappointment. The kid was still young, and Connor could only hope he'd bounce back with the next changes in his life. Sacrifices had to be made to become successful. Unfortunately, Trey's wants, or at least what his son *thought* he wanted, would be one of them.

Once the kid was out on the road, he'd change his mind. Who wouldn't become all-consumed with the thrill of traveling with the team, city to city, chasing the dream?

"Hey, Hank. Didn't you shower this morning? You stink like a donkey," one of the seasoned players on the team shouted, dissing one of the rookies a couple of rows up.

"Shut up. I didn't have time. I was too busy out with the ladies while you were home in bed, daddy-o." The kid's long and unruly hair, blue eyes, and tanned skin were sure to earn him his fair share of the lady pool. Though what they would see when the kid talked was his immaturity—something Connor was tasked with fixing.

"Whatever, moron. At least I have someone at home." Randy was one of the older players on the team and the most settled. He was lucky to have a wife who supported his career.

"That would be a boring life for an up-and-coming rock star." The kid was all talk, but his attitude would have a serious change over the next few weeks and months. That is if he wanted to play ball. Rookie versus pro prompted quite a few of the razzings that occurred, and other more direct attacks were centered on pure jealousy.

Connor had forgotten this part of the road trips. Grown men that needed babysitting—only now *he* was the babysitter. Trying to drown out their useless banter, he pulled out his phone and checked his email. His gaze landed on the one from two days ago. He clicked on the email and scrolled through the photos Lynette had sent. *Trey laughing as he and Gabby were walking across the field. Gabby on the pitching mound. Trey at bat.* It reminded him of the evening they'd all gone out. He flipped to his photo album and found one of his favorites. *Lynette in the outfield, hands and glove in the air, trying to catch the ball.* As luck would have it, it turned out to be her first catch. Even if you couldn't tell it in the photo—Connor knew.

He scrolled through more of the photos, ones of the middle school ball team at practice and at the games. Connor glanced out the window. Mile markers flew by, one by one. He'd missed his son's most exciting game—just like his own father had done repeatedly.

Connor didn't want to be like his father, but what else could he do? He replayed the video clip he'd save, relishing in his son's joy. He was proud of Trey. And Connor had missed the moment and the shared joy. It was a moment he'd never get back.

Loud laughter caught his attention as the guys were roughhousing at the front of the bus. Some were singing, some told stupid jokes, some boastful and arrogant, ready to be the new star. It was the same and yet different. The same because it was familiar. Different because he wasn't sure he was a part of the action, or more specifically, that he wanted to be a part of this lifestyle.

The thrill wasn't there. Maybe all it would take was to get back into the game action. Hear the roar of the crowds as they cheered their favorite teams and players. At least, he hoped that was the case. Either that, or he'd just made the biggest mistake of his life walking away from Trey. And Gabby...his pitching protégé. *And Lynette.* The woman he'd fallen in love with. He was sure of it now. Talk about blindsided. But it was the only explanation for the empty feeling in his gut, knowing he was leaving behind all the most important people in his life. And for what?

Life on the road.

Chapter Eighteen

♥

AFTER A SLEEPLESS NIGHT filled with tossing and turning, Connor finally gave in to the need for caffeine. He found the coffee maker, added a pod, and headed for the bathroom to get some water in the little paper cup provided—one of the not-so-luxury benefits of a cheaper hotel. The off-brand would either taste like mud or water, but anything would be fine at this point if it woke him up artificially.

He rubbed his eyes, wiping away the sleep dirt from the corners. Glancing over at the other occupant in the room, he noted the young kid was still sound asleep. Some of the trouble sleeping originated from his roommates snoring, the rest thinking about the people he cared about that he'd left behind in Hallbrook.

His son's unhappy attitude weighed heavily on Connor's mind. Going into the bathroom, coffee cup in hand, he shut the door and leaned against the counter. Pulling out his phone, he shifted the volume down so as not to wake his roommate. He cued up the video of his son hitting the home run that took the team to today's championship game.

The game he would miss.

Connor absorbed the sights and sounds, letting the feeling wash over him as he tried to bask in his son's glory. The bleachers were filled with excited parents, all hoping to be part of the winning team. Supportive parents, no matter the outcome of the game but hoping their child emerged victorious at the end of seven innings.

It was a time when memories were made. Or, in his case, memories missed. Lynette's words kept ringing in his head as he watched the video. *There's no shame in making it to the minors. Only a handful of people move on to the majors. It's all about timing and opportunity. A better message for Trey would be to show him that family is more important than proving your worth at all costs.*

At all costs.

As if thinking about her conjured up her image, Connor noticed Lynette in the background of the video. Something he hadn't seen before—his eyes always on the foreground and Trey at bat. He watched as she jumped up and down in excitement, high-fiving the other kids on the team, joy in every move she made. The kids rushing out of the dugout to watch Trey round the bases. The team surrounded him, Keith picking him up and putting him on his shoulders.

Like a father and son.

Except Trey was his son.

In this business, you could be riding high, and the next day, be on your way home. Whether as a player or a coach, it could be fleeting. But his son was there for the long haul. Connor closed his eyes to the images as they started to blur. He had failed the most important person in his life in his selfish quest for fame and glory. He should have been there to share in the moment—just like he should be there now.

Not trusting his heart was his biggest mistake yet. It was time to fight for love and family. Something more fulfilling than a lonely road job. Instead of proving himself in baseball, he should have been proving himself as a good father—and that meant putting his son first.

He thought he'd be a fool not to jump at the chance to coach, but the truth was, he'd been a fool to give up everything good in his life to go after an old dream. It was something he had to fix.

While he still could.

Connor glanced at his watch, an idea forming and taking hold. The championship game was at two. The biggest game of the season, and he was stuck in Chicago to coach a bunch of overgrown rookie wannabes instead of with his son. The thrill of helping these guys had faded the minute he'd been thrust back into the arena and had to sit on the bus for hours listening to the players' cocky attitudes.

Watching his son play ball had brought him far more joy. Not to mention coaching Gabby and watching her get better and better every day as she learned new pitches and gained confidence.

The same was true of Lynette. Kissing her straw-berry-flavored lips and spending time watching her laugh brought him a depth of joy previously unknown. She embraced life head-on with a zest long denied in a life of chaos.

The same couldn't be said about his life when he was in the minors. Why hadn't he understood the true joys in his life before now? Baseball wasn't what made him happy, life with Trey did that. And if he hadn't destroyed all his chances with Lynette, he could have her and Gabby in his life also.

It was only seven a.m. There were still seven hours until the championship game—minus one hour for time zone changes. He nodded, knowing he could just about make it before the first pitch was thrown with any luck—but it all depended on him catching a direct flight out of Chicago this morning.

Connor reached for the door handle, needing to pack. *Was he crazy?* This would mean giving up everything he'd worked for all his life. *No.* It meant he finally put family first, something he should have done throughout Trey's life. He'd missed so much, and he didn't want to miss another day. The chance to make another happy memory.

He tossed his duffel bag on the bed, making sure to pick up all his belongings. Taking a deep breath, he pulled up his airline search app, typing in his information.

Bingo. He chuckled, the word making him think of Lynette's dog. Another outgoing, live-life-to-the-fullest member of the Taylor family.

There was a non-stop flight from Chicago to Logan International Airport in Boston. Connor pressed the book button before giving himself time to change his mind. He was really going to do this.

The confirmation email pinged his phone, and he let out a deep breath. The hardest part came next. He pulled up his email app and started to type. The more he typed, the faster it went, the words pouring out of him, cleansing his heart and soul. This was a new beginning, and the resignation letter left him feeling more free, happy, and light-hearted than he could have imagined.

It's not as if he was giving up baseball. He'd still coach his son's teams and help Trey and Gabby. And with Lynette and the kids filling his life with true and meaningful joy, he would consider himself blessed.

Connor pressed send. After booking transportation to the airport, he headed out the door. His roommate hadn't stirred and Connor didn't feel the need to wake him. He'd find out in due time what was going on.

Soon the city buildings gave way to the outskirts of town. It wasn't long before the driver dropped him off at the departure gate area. Connor wound his way through the complicated terminal, went through security, and then followed the signs to his gate. It wasn't long before they boarded the plane and were waiting for take off. Using the extra time, he booked a rental car from Logan International and hoped everything went well, and that he wouldn't be too late for the start of the game.

Better late than never. Connor hoped the old adage was true.

Gabby and Trey sat glumly at the kitchen table, picking at the pancakes Lynette had whipped up for today's special occasion. She had hoped her efforts would have lightened the mood, considering she'd even made each pancake like a baseball, using whip cream and licorice strings to decorate each one. Even Bingo lay nearby, his head down as if sensing the mood.

"What's with all the long faces?" Keith asked, entering the kitchen.

Trey shrugged, poking at the food on his plate.

"It's not the same without Coach," Gabby said, shooting a glance at Trey.

Keith frowned, shaking his head. "Okay, so what? You just give up. Connor had a job to do, and he's doing it. The same way you both have a job to do. And anything worth doing is worth giving it your all."

"Keith's right. You both need to perk up. Show the team what you're made of. Sugar and spice and everything nice," she teased, trying to push the kids out of the funk they were in.

Trey shoved his plate back, having barely touched the pancakes. "But what if we lose? My dad will be disappointed in me. And he can tell me how he would have done it differently since he's the expert and all. And what does it matter anyway? He's still going to make me leave. What's the point?" The kid had a huge chip on his shoulder, and only Connor could fix it. Too bad he wasn't here. Her heart ached for the boy who seemed lost.

"It doesn't matter if you win or lose as long as you try your best. That's all your dad wants you to do. It's what he's doing. I'm sure he hates missing your game again, but he's doing his best to make everything work. And since when has he ever talked down about the way you play? You should cut him some slack. Besides, Lynette and I have put a lot into this team also, and we'll be there to cheer you on. Just like all the other parents who can make the game. Some parents will have to work and miss it. It's just the way life goes sometimes." Mr. Motivational was working his magic, and Lynette was more than happy to let him take over.

"I reckon." Trey shrugged again.

Keith sat down at the table and pushed Trey's plate closer. "Eat up, both of you. We've got to leave early today to help line the fields, and I want the team to warm up a bit before we officially start." He wasn't taking no for an answer.

"Okay," they said in unison.

Lynette was surprised to see them start to eat, their attitudes changing right before her eyes.

They polished off their plates and headed down the hall to get ready. Thinking about the game, they'd been unable to stop the anticipation of the big day, Keith's words on point. "Thanks, Keith. I wasn't sure what to say."

Keith shrugged. "Sometimes it's not what you say, but how you say it. They needed to focus on what was important, and right now, that's the game. Not Connor's absence."

Too bad Lynette couldn't heed Keith's words. She was also missing Connor and he hadn't been gone but a day. Perhaps it was simply knowing the decision to end their short relationship wasn't temporary, and no number of days that went by would change the result. Even talking to him would have made things better, but she'd messed up and ended everything, even any chance at a friendship. Her knee-jerk reaction was one she now regretted.

By the time they loaded up and headed for the ballfield, Lynette was a nervous wreck.

"Why don't you two help carry some of the equipment to the field, and then you can go chat with some of the other kids as they start to arrive?" Keith suggested.

"Sure thing, Uncle Keith," Gabby said.

"And remember, be confident. Show them your heart is in this game and that you care. Lead by example."

"Yes, sir," Trey answered as he picked up the bag of baseballs and headed for the field.

Gabby grabbed the extra gloves, the box with the record book, and the field chalk, before she started to walk away.

Lynette grabbed her daughter's arm. "You okay, Gabby?"

"Sure thing. Coach taught me a lot, but you and Uncle Keith are right. I don't need him to do my best—I'll just do it."

Lynette flinched. It was the right attitude but with the wrong emotion. *Anger.*

"Honey, it'll be okay. I promise." She hugged her daughter briefly, trying to reassure her and hoping she'd redirect some of the negative energy. It wouldn't help if she took it out on the mound.

"We'll know soon enough," Gabby said, walking away to join the others who had started to arrive.

"Sounds like we need to give a pep talk to the whole team. I wish Connor hadn't left them like this a second time," Keith said, frowning as he watched his niece walk away.

Lynette nodded. "I agree. But it's like you said, the job was a good opportunity and one he couldn't very well say no to. It's his future and coaching the school baseball team, isn't." She was trying her hardest to put on a game face for the kids but judging by her brother's hard gaze, he wasn't buying her false bravado.

"You miss him, don't you?" he asked.

It wasn't any use trying to avoid the question. Her brother knew her too well. "Yes. I mean, what's not to miss? He's good with the kids and the team."

"That's not what I meant, and you know it. I saw the way the two of you looked at each other," Keith said by way of prompting her to reveal the truth.

"I care about him if that's what you're asking. But it's a friendship, nothing more. Or it was. We left things on not-so-good terms."

Keith snickered. "Whatever. I don't think the sudden spark of life and the glow on your face when you talk about him has anything to do with a friendship. And whatever it is, it's certainly not over."

Lynette shrugged. Her brother didn't understand, and if she wanted this interrogation to end, it was up to her to end it. "It doesn't matter. He made his choice, and it's not a life I want. End of story."

"So you are interested. And you can make anything work if you put your heart into it." Keith grinned as he grabbed the last duffel bag from the back of the truck and swung it over his shoulder.

"*Was* interested. It's just not that easy." It was the same thing she'd thought, but it didn't change a thing. Connor was gone, and his departure hadn't come with any promises to return and pick up where they left off.

"Make it easy. Connor's not Dirk, so don't make the mistake of lumping them together. It doesn't have to be all one way or the other. Talk to Connor, Lynette. You owe it to yourself. It's the same thing you've been telling Trey. Maybe it's time you practice what you preach." She knew he was right, but it wouldn't make it any easier.

"Maybe. Right now, we've got a game to coach." They each grabbed one side of the water cooler and started for the dugout. It was heavy, and the weight of Keith's words made it heavier.

"What's going on over there?" Keith asked, pointing at the kids. They had all formed a group around Trey, listening to whatever he had to say.

"I don't know, and there's only one way to find out." They dropped the cooler off near the dugout and headed in the kid's direction.

"We owe it to ourselves to play our best. Forget everything else except the game. Let's win today because we're the best, and we've earned the right to be here. Let's give it everything we've got, so that no matter whether we win or lose, we know we gave it our best shot." Trey was in the middle of a motivational speech to the team, and Lynette couldn't be prouder of the boy. He'd take Keith's words to heart and was living them and breathing life into the rest of the team. The kid was stepping up as the captain of the team and sounding very much like his father.

"Guess we can cross pep talk off our list," Keith said, grinning over at her.

"So it would seem. Thank you."

"Anytime, sis," he said, bumping her shoulder.

The team warmed up while Keith and Lynette lined the field. By the time the umps showed up,

Lynette was a nervous wreck. The head ump blew the whistle, and both teams jogged off the field, back to their dugouts.

Let the game begin.

Chapter Nineteen

♥

"SHAKE IT OFF, RILEY. It's okay," Lynette said, trying to encourage the boy after his last pitch. Unfortunately, it had gone right down the strike zone into the sweet spot, allowing the batter to dig in deep and come up with a home run, driving in another runner. The game was tied at 2 - 2 at the top of the third inning.

Riley nodded, a grim look on his face. He settled into position, his back straight, wound up, and fired, the pitch going wildly to the left and into the backstop. Another foot left, and it would have been into the crowd of onlookers.

"Ball," the ump called out. Luckily, Tommy caught the wild throw, which kept the other team from scoring another run.

She looked back at Riley, only to discover him clutching his pitching shoulder. Coming out of the dugout, she made eye contact with the ump. "Time out," she called.

He threw his hand in the air and blew the whistle, signaling he'd heard and acknowledged the request for her to go out on the field. Lynette jogged to the pitcher's mound, Keith coming in from third base where he'd been coaching the kids.

"What's wrong?" she asked, taking the ball from Riley.

The kid looked as if he'd like to ignore the question, but in the end, he grabbed his shoulder just as a pained expression crossed his face. "I don't know. It hurt real bad when I threw the last ball. It started as twitches of pain, but each pitch gets worse. This last one, it felt like it pulled or something." He kicked the dirt on the mound, trying to keep a brave face.

Giving up the mound at this point in the game would be hard for the boy, but they had to go with what was best for him and the team. There was no way she wanted to chance him tearing something. "We need to get you to the medical center and let

Dr. Duncan look at it. Wouldn't want to take any chances on making it worse."

"But I don't want to leave the game," he said, scuffing the ground again with his foot. "Gabby can't pitch that many innings. We'll lose for sure," he added, a scowl on his face.

"I don't think we have a choice, Riley," Keith jumped in, backing up her decision.

The kid was right about Gabby not having pitched this many innings. She was the backup pitcher for the team, but she was about to face her biggest challenge yet.

"I'll explain what's going on to your parents. They can get you to a doctor and, hopefully, back here in time to watch the game and cheer your teammates on," Lynette said, handing the ball to her brother. "Keith, can you let the ump know the change we're making and explain what's going on?"

"Will do," her brother said, walking toward home plate.

"It's not fair," Riley mumbled.

"You did well out there, Riley. But right now, you can't give us your best. Show some faith in Gabby's abilities. You know she's good. She just needs more confidence," Lynette said, waiting for Riley to voluntarily go off the field with her.

"Fine," he said, his hung head low. At least he was leaving without making a scene.

"Gabby," she hollered, signaling for her daughter to head to the mound.

Her daughter ran out, slowing as she drew near. "Is he going to be okay?" she asked, biting down on her lower lip. It had always been a telltale sign of her nerves.

"Yes. I'm sure of it, but we need you to pitch," Lynette said, hoping Riley wouldn't sound off and make the situation more tense. "Just remember to breathe out there."

"Sure thing," Gabby said, renewing the lower lip bite.

"You got this, Gabby. You can do it. You're one heck of a pitcher, and I wouldn't want anyone else to replace me. Bring this home for the team," Riley said, nodding and sending Gabby a smile.

"Sure thing. Like, no pressure, right?" Gabby seemed equally surprised by the kid's words, but now wasn't the time to question anything. Her daughter had a game to pitch.

Riley shrugged. "Try the underwear thing. I used it, and it really works." He held his arm as if another shot of pain had caught him off guard.

"*Ewww*. Thanks, but no thanks." Gabby chuckled.

"Then try picturing them dressed as clowns," Lynette suggested, needing to get a move on for multiple reasons.

"Gotcha. I can live with that image," Gabby said. "Thanks, Riley." She nodded and headed for the mound.

Lynette was proud of her daughter for stepping up in the face of pressure. She was equally proud of Riley for encouraging her. The team had grown close over the past month, and the team-building skills had really paid off. Win or lose, the Legal Eagles were winners in her books.

After a quick chat with Riley's parents, Lynette headed back to the dugout.

"What's going on?" Teddy, one of the youngest players on the team asked the question she was sure everyone wanted to be answered.

"Riley hurt his arm. His parents are taking him to the medical center as a precaution, but I think he'll be fine. Might have pulled something," Lynette said, trying to reassure the kid and the others who'd gathered around. "Make sure we cheer loud and proud for the team. It's up to us to get their heads back in the game and let them know we believe in them, with or without Riley."

"Okay, Principal Taylor. We got this," one of the other kids said. They all lined up along the chain-link fence and started cheering as Gabby finished her warmup pitches.

Gabby glanced in her direction. Lynette nodded, hoping to reassure her. She'd never pitched four innings before, and the toll it would take on her arm was no small feat.

Lynette had faith in her. Now, it was up to Gabby to have faith in herself.

Her first pitch went wide. As did her second. Lynette held her breath, fully aware of her daughter's level of tension. It showed in every part of the pitch—nothing smooth in her delivery.

The catcher threw the ball back to first base after Gabby walked the batter. Trey caught it and walked to the pitcher's mound, placing the ball in Gabby's glove. He said something to her, and then returned to the plate.

Whatever he said seemed to work, Gabby's next pitch was a strike. And then another. With only two more singles and no runs scored, they cleared the inning. By the time they reached the bottom of the fifth, Lynette could tell Gabby was tired from pitching, but through it all, her daughter held her own. Next in the batting line-up, her daughter's lip biting had grown more pronounced as she took to the field. Her batting skill wasn't her strong suit, and Lynette couldn't help but say a little prayer.

Gabby choked up on the bat and swung, missing high. Her second swing connected, barely, as it rolled back toward the pitcher, just wide enough to make him run. She took off like a steam engine, barreling toward first base as if her life depended on it. The pitcher tried to grab the ball, missed the first time, and managed to pick it up and throw to first base.

"Safe," the ump called, gesturing with his arms to make sure everyone knew the call.

Gabby dusted off her pants and shirt from where she'd slid into the base and looked over at the team, grinning as they all clapped and cheered. Two batters later, and with two outs against them, Trey stepped up to the plate, the score still 2 - 2.

"Come on, son. You got this!"

Lynette heard the voice and the words but couldn't wrap her head around them. She swung around, coming face to face with Connor. "You're here," she said, stunned and unable to put together much more than two simple words.

"I am," Connor said, his charming smile firmly in place. "Sorry, I'm a little late. I was a bit delayed."

"Coach, you're here," the other kids said, gathering around.

Connor stepped out of the dugout, making sure Trey saw him. He clapped and cheered when his son swung, fouling the ball past third base.

"You got this. Way to see the ball," Connor called out.

Trey grinned and nodded, suddenly looking not only like a leader in command of the ball team, but a happy one. *Relaxed*. He swung the bat a few times and stepped back up to the plate. After settling in, the pitcher threw a fastball, Trey swung. The crack of the bat and the sight of the ball flying over the heads of the outfielders told the whole story.

Home run.

Lynette's eyes blurred as she watched the scene unfold. Connor ran down the field toward first plate, clapping and cheering his support as Trey rounded the bases. With Gabby coming home, the score was now 4 - 2. They had a long way to go, but it would give everyone some breathing room.

Trey and Gabby came toward the dugout, the team rushing out to meet and high-five each other before returning to the bench.

"Great job, both of you," Lynette said, patting Trey on the shoulder and hugging Gabby.

Connor high-fived his son. "Guess I made it just in time."

"I can't believe you're here," Trey said, a wide smile on his face. Now *that* was one happy kid.

"Neither can I," Lynette chimed in.

Connor shrugged. "I'll explain later. Right now, we've got a ball game to win. Let's go, team!"

Lynette didn't want to wait until later. Connor's presence had set her heart to racing and left her confused. He was supposed to be in Chicago, and she couldn't begin to figure out why he was here. But no matter what the reason, she was happy about it. Connor Weston was right where he belonged in her books.

The next batter struck out, and the Legal Eagles went back onto the field.

Connor picked up Gabby's glove off the bench and handed it to her. "You've got this, Gabby. Show them what you're made of."

"Right, Coach." She grinned, running onto the field.

Both teams had brought their A-game. It was the top of the seventh, and the Eagles were ahead by one run. Gabby was tired and running out of steam but holding steady. Connor had taken over coaching, and Lynette was happy to be back in the role of team mom, encouraging the kids and making sure they stayed hydrated. Keith continued to monitor third base, and the team's spirits stayed high.

Unlike Lynette's nerves—which were frazzled. She wanted the team to win, and they were so close, but the pressure on Gabby was more than her daughter could handle. It's not like she had experience pulling out all stops on the back end of a long game. Not to mention, Connor's presence had sent Lynette into a tailspin.

Gabby pitched, fierce determination etched on her face. Three strikes later, she retired the batter, ready to face the next one. The confident kid stepped up to the plate, not even bothering to take a few practice swings. He swung and missed.

"Strike," the ump called. Two strikes later, the kid wasn't smiling.

One more out and they would win the game. Gabby looked to Connor for support. He nodded and sent her a signal, to which she nodded in return. Something was up between them, but she trusted they knew what they were doing with the game on the line.

Gabby sent a sinkerball across the plate, the kid swinging and missing high. The next pitch flew in high, and the kid swung and missed low. Her daughter took a few deep breaths and settled into position.

Lynette held her breath as her daughter wound up and pitched. The kid swung the bat into position for a bunt, the ball striking the sweet spot and heading straight for Gabby. The player took off running as her daughter fielded the ball, grabbing it with her right hand, turned, and threw it to first base. It was going to be close.

"Out," the ump called, throwing his hand to give the signal so everyone understood the call.

The whole team had done it, and she was proud of her daughter's part in the win. No one would doubt her ability ever again. Lynette couldn't stop the tears from streaming down her face as the team rushed in. Connor rushed out to meet Gabby, lifting her up onto his shoulders. He carried her back to the dugout, one arm around Trey as the team all rushed together in centerfield.

The kids hugged and high-fived as the other team walked off the field.

Minutes later, the two teams lined up to do the good-game routine. It had been an excellent game, and both groups of kids had played rock solid. She was proud of Trey when he went over and shook hands with the other team's coach, following Connor's lead and showing his respect.

Keith and Lynette waited by the dugout, cleaning up some of the trash lying around.

"Pizza at Sally's for all. On me," Keith called out to the parents standing close by, waiting to congratulate the boys and Gabby. Everyone cheered, teasing each other as they headed for the parking lot.

The Legal Eagles had done it. They'd won the school's first championship game.

Next stop, state finals.

The only question that remained was, who would be their coach?

The celebration party at Sally's had lasted for two hours, the kids and their parents practically overrunning the place. His son was the happiest Connor ever remembered seeing. The joy of being victorious was part of it, but it wasn't all of it.

Connor would never forget the surprise or the love he'd seen in Trey's eyes when he heard him call out his encouragement, letting his son know he was there. He knew without a doubt that he had done the right thing by coming home.

And then there was Gabby. She'd come a long way from when she first arrived, her outgoing confidence a joy to watch. Being here now to celebrate with the kids and the team made everything he'd given up worth it and then some.

Herbert Farnsworth had emailed him back, disappointed in his decision, but surprisingly, he understood. They would move forward with their second-choice person for the job, and life just went on—with or without him.

The party at Sally's gave him the time to figure out what he wanted to say to Lynette and how to say it. Pouring his heart out wouldn't come easy, but it was necessary. He'd done enough damage to their relationship, and it was past time he stepped up to the plate. *For her.*

He wouldn't blame Lynette if she wasn't interested, considering the way he'd walked away without so much as a backward glance. If only she the truth—it had been way more than a backward glance. His heart hadn't let go and had kept her close through photos and remembering all the fun they'd had together. He hadn't let go—not by a long shot.

Connor took Lynette by the hand and led her to the back patio, the kids still in the living room with

Keith talking up a storm. "Finally, we're alone. I know today's been action-packed, but I also know you've got questions. Questions I'm ready to answer."

Lynette stepped back, putting a little distance between them. "Good. I can't imagine how you pulled off getting here in time, but I'm glad you did. Also, I'm trying to figure out why."

He didn't blame her...but he had hoped it wasn't too late to fix what went wrong. "It's called a non-stop flight. And as to why, that's easy. Trey and Gabby had a championship game to play, and I'm the coach. This is where I should have been all along. I made a mistake walking away like I did, and I want to try and fix thing. I couldn't stop thinking about all of you."

Lynette smiled. "I see. It was good, you coming back, I mean. And since it would seem it's time for confessions, I've got one as well. I'm sorry I shut you out the way I did. You see, you weren't the only one making a mistake. I know you weren't gone but a day, but I missed talking to you. It felt empty not knowing I could pick up the phone and call, just to hear your voice, or to laugh about the day or the antics of the kids. I missed you." Her voice had dropped to a whisper, but he heard her—loud and clear.

Even if he hadn't, his heart had, the sudden pounding in his chest proof. "That's good." He grinned, taking her hand again and pulling her closer.

"It is?" she asked softly.

Connor wanted to get this right. "Yes. Relationships require sacrifice to make them work."

"I agree, and I'm sorry I wasn't willing to try before," Lynette added, moving closer still.

Connor let out a deep sigh. "It's not you, trust me. I was trying to make life's successes into the basis of relationships. With my father. My son. You. I've been so focused on chasing a dream, I've missed sight of what was most important in my life. I hope you can forgive me for being such a fool." He entwined her fingers in his, needing the contact.

Lynette nodded, her beautiful smile bringing warmth to his heart. "I'm ready to face whatever you need to do as a coach, as long as we face it together. I promise to be more flexible and try to make whatever this is between us work if you let me."

This was commitment. It was what he had been missing in his life. Someone to love him, for him. Not what he could do, or how high he could rise, but just for him. Lynette was willing to do whatever he needed as long as they were together. What she didn't know yet, was that she was his life. Wherever she and the kids were, is where Connor wanted to be. "The only flexibility I want from you is to know you'll travel with the team when necessary," he said, grinning and savoring the moment.

Lynette's smile faltered. "I was thinking more of staying here in Hallbrook, and we work it out. I might be able to arrange some travel, but I have the children and my job to think about. I'm just not saying no to us," she clarified.

His grin grew wider, his cheeks aching. "I meant traveling with the Legal Eagles to the state finals. And maybe even a camping trip or two thrown in for good measure. I seem to recall you agreed to one that's coming up soon. That's still on, I presume." He'd almost forgotten the Father's Day camping trip, but it was another bonus to coming home.

And Connor had no intentions of letting her off the hook.

"I don't understand. What do you mean?" she asked.

The moment of truth was upon him. "I quit the coaching job with the minor league. My job is to be the best PE teacher I can be and to coach the Legal Eagles. That is, *if* my job is still available."

Lynette frowned. "Why would you quit? You worked hard for this." Her reaction wasn't what he expected, and was more than a little concerning. Had he been wrong about her and that his status with the ball club did matter?

All in. He'd promised himself this much, and he wasn't walking away without a fight. "Like I said, some things are more important. Trey. Gabby. And you." Connor leaned forward and kissed her, loving the strawberry flavor he'd come to enjoy and missed, even if it had only been a day and a half. "This life is my first and last choice. The dream I once had doesn't exist anymore, and a new dream has taken its place. Life with you and the kids is what I want more than anything in the world."

Lynette smiled, wrapping her arms around his neck. "I think I can handle the job of principal and team mom, thank you very much." She grinned. "Especially if my reward is your kisses. Consider it my payment of sorts."

Thank you, God. He'd been blessed with multitudes of love. "I like the sound of that."

"And yes, the job is still open. Lucky for you, it's summer," Lynette said, grinning.

"Works for me. Should we go break the news to the kids? Trey will be thrilled, I suspect," Connor said, taking Lynette by the arm and leading her inside.

"I second that suspicion. And Gabby's going to be right there with him. She's grown far more attached to you than I could have believed possible in such a short time."

"She's a great kid and a great pitcher. We have a lot in common," he teased, dropping another kiss on Lynette's lips.

Lynette laughed and shook her head. "I see your ego hasn't changed."

"Nope. It comes with the territory."

"Well, okay then since I like the territory. Oh, and one other little thing. Do we have to go camping? I'd rather we compromise on that and not go."

"That's not compromising. Besides, you have already agreed to go again, you can't back out now. Maybe you'll fall in love with camping the same way I'm hoping you'll fall in love with me." Call it testing the waters or insanity, but Connor didn't mind dropping the *L* word. He wasn't ready to say it yet, but he was close. And if things worked out, they'd have the rest of their lives to say it. For now, he wanted to make sure they both had a chance to explore their feelings and decide if it was the real and lasting kind of love.

"I guess anything is possible when you put it that way," she teased.

"Does that mean that maybe you have already? Fallen, that is," he clarified, unable to hold back the rush of feeling as he considered the possibility.

"Are you asking about camping or you?" Lynette asked, a teasing light in her eyes.

"Me," he said, pausing in the doorway to hear her answer. *Just in case.*

"Maybe. I'm working on it. Guess you'll have to stick around to find out."

Connor couldn't believe it.

Baseball had been his dream, but it never left him feeling this good about life.

Chapter Twenty

♥

"CAR'S PACKED. EVERYBODY READY to go?" Lynette called out, unsure where the kids had gotten off to. Voices trickled down the hall, and she followed the sound.

It was no surprise that while she and Connor had been packing, the kids had been playing video games. For as much as they'd become the best of teammates on the ballfield, they were huge competitors in every other way. "Come on, you two. Let's get a move on."

"We're coming, Mom," Gabby said, even as she continued to twist and turn and use the remote control, unwilling to concede even a few seconds.

"I'm going to unplug it on the count of three. One, two, th..."

The screen went blank. "Fine," Trey said, rolling his eyes as he glanced up at her and stood.

"If you all don't want to go to the lake, you could always stay here with my brother." She knew it was an empty threat. This camping trip was all they talked about for the past two weeks.

"No way," they both said, right on cue.

They made it as far as the living room when Connor came through the front door.

"Load up," he said. "Time to go."

Bingo raced out the open door, making sure he wouldn't be left behind.

"I get passenger side," Trey called out.

"You got it last time," Gabby said, racing ahead to the truck.

"Did not. Besides, it's our truck, smarty pants."

"Did too." Gabby beat him to the truck and pulled open the door, climbing inside after Bingo jumped in.

"Dad, tell her to slide over." Trey had been hampered down by his backpack, something that should have already been in the truck. This was one argument Lynette intended to stay out of, especially since it happened every time the four of them went anywhere.

Connor, on the other hand, was being dragged into it. "I think she's right about who had it last time, son. Sorry." Neither of them liked sitting behind Connor when he drove because his seat had to go all the way back to accommodate his long legs.

"Whatever," Trey said, tossing his backpack in the truck bed and climbing up into the back seat.

The trip might have been planned for a year, but four people hadn't been on the original agenda. Unlucky for her, but then, she'd promised Connor to try and enjoy this trip. And he was right—she was more prepared. Not to mention, Connor had bought a new tent for the occasion. It was to replace the pup tent, his thought that they should have two large tents making perfect sense. One for the guys and one for the girls, but each one big enough to hold their belongings. He'd even picked out a cot and foam pad to put under her sleeping bag, hoping to make it more comfortable. It was all part of his plan to make her fall in love with camping, not that she held out hope his plan would work.

The only thing Lynette was expecting to fall in love with, was Connor himself. Especially since she was fairly certain she was already in love with him. They'd agreed to commit to a relationship to see where things would go and had spent almost every day for the past two weeks together. There hadn't been much alone time, other than a few dinner dates and one candlelight dinner Connor had cooked at his place. Gabby and Trey had gone out to eat with Keith. Life with kids was always busy, and even though chaotic at times, it was chaos she enjoyed because they were together—like a family.

Connor had a way of making her feel special, something she missed for about the last five years of her marriage. She had fallen in love with Dirk, but he had fallen in love with the military life. Now, it was nice to come first and to have someone to share the responsibility of raising children with.

The kids were busy playing games on their cell phones, which was fine with Lynette. Watching them together, one would swear they were already brother and sister, judging by the constant picking.

"I'm glad we are finally getting away. From work, school, everything," Connor said, reaching for her hand.

"Even baseball?" she teased.

"Absolutely. With the state finals coming up, we'll have lots of practice, but for now—it's just you, me, and the kids."

"And the snakes, animals, and bugs," she said, scrunching up her face. Connor rented kayaks again, and the thought of paddling around with the squiggly, slimy reptiles wasn't high on her priority list. Her preference would be to sit that activity out and take Bingo on a long walk instead. Somehow, she wasn't sure she'd be able to get out of the paddle trip, but it wouldn't stop her from trying.

"All much smaller than you. And more afraid of you than you are of them. I promise," he said, trying to reassure her but failing miserably.

"Tell that to the mosquitoes. I think they failed to get the message." She laughed. Time would tell whether she'd ever be a fan of camping, but she would give it her best shot.

Connor looked over at her and grinned. "You're just too sweet to resist."

"Really, you two. We are just kids," Gabby said.

"And we can hear you," Trey chimed in. Proof they weren't as wrapped up into their games as once thought.

"We need a divider glass to block out all the romantic mumble-jumble you too insist on saying," Gabby added.

Her daughter was totally okay with her and Connor in a relationship. It was just the occasional kiss she minded. And the hugs. And the hand holding. Apparently, that stuff was for younger, non-parental folks.

They tried to limit their PDA when the kids were around, not wanting to embarrass them. People around town had become used to seeing them together. Connor had been right, the newest item on the gossip chain having replaced them.

"We're here, so I guess you can help unload, and then you won't have to listen," Connor teased, pulling up to the registration booth. He rolled down the window. "Good afternoon. Connor Weston. Site C14."

"Welcome to White Mountain State Park." The park ranger flipped through a box of passes. And yes, I've got you right here, Mr. Weston." The woman handed him a parking pass and a map. "We're full this week. Consider yourself lucky you booked in advance and managed to show up before the rush. Another hour and the line to get in will be backed up to the main road."

Connor smiled. "Yes. We love to camp here, and I learned the routine early on. Father's Day week is always booked solid."

The young woman nodded, her smile cheery. "There's a list of activities stapled to the map. Be sure to check it out. Lots of great things for the kids to get involved with."

"Sounds like a plan." Connor drove into the park and made his way to the C loop. "Wait till you see the site. It may change your idea about camping right on the spot."

"What? Is it a cabin with a kitchen, a bathroom, and a bedroom?" Lynette teased, knowing it wasn't true.

Connor chuckled. "Close enough. There's a fire-place, restrooms, and a tent."

"Doesn't sound any different to me from the last one."

Connor pulled into the site, and Lynette was blown away by what she saw. "Now, what do you think?" he asked.

Lynette got out of the truck. "It's gorgeous." A waterfront campsite with the sunlight shimmering off the water. The backdrop mountains and lake as far as the eye could see. Lots of blue sky, an occasional cloud, and lots of boaters out on the water. She walked down the path to the water's edge, the kids close on her heels.

"This is really cool," Gabby said. "Can we go swimming? Like from right here, or do we have to go to the beach?"

Trey picked up a rock and tossed it in the water, Bingo trying to chase it and managing to go for a little swim. "Right here. Nice, huh? Dad and I timed the reservation so we could get this spot. It's one of the best in the park. He stayed up till midnight the night before the reservations opened for this day, just to get it first."

The fact Connor had gone to such lengths was more proof his heart had always been in the right place when it came to his son. He'd just needed his brain to catch up. Lucky for her, it had happened in time for the two of them to figure things out. It was a true blessing.

"This is incredible," Lynette said, leaning over to touch the water. "It's cold, though. Not sure who's going to be swimming, but it won't be me." Bingo ran up next to her as he came out of the water, but she was unable to back away in time. The dog shook, spraying cold water all over her. "Stoppp," she cried out, not that it would have any effect.

The others laughed. "If you sit out in the sun long enough, you'll want to jump in," Connor said, skipping a rock across the surface of the lake.

Lynette shook her head. "But then there's the snakes who want to do the same thing. I'll pass." She frowned.

"I'll protect you." Connor grinned and grabbed her hand to help her back up the path to the gravel pad where they needed to set up camp. "So what do you think? Lakefront real estate for the price of an overnight stay."

"I like it—a lot. Thanks for sharing this with us. You know, with it being Father's Day weekend and all," she added, still feeling a little guilty for stepping in on a special time for him and Trey.

"Father's Day weekend isn't just for fathers and sons. It's for family. Trust me, I've got something special planned for this week, and Trey will be over the moon."

Connor hadn't said a thing to her about plans beyond kayaking, but special sounded good to her no matter what it was. *Okay, so within reason, she corrected.*

"What is it, Dad?" Trey asked.

Connor turned to face them all, his excitement obvious as the charming smile Lynette loved, lit his face. "Well, instead of kayaks, I rented a pontoon boat for the whole week. We've got to pick it up after we get the tents set up, and then I can drive it back here and park it at the site. That way, we can fish anytime, cruise anytime, and go anywhere on the lake."

"Cool," Trey said, nodding. "This will be awesome."

"Awesome, Coach," Gabby added, seconding Trey's reaction. The nickname "Coach" had stuck, and it removed any awkwardness her daughter had been feeling in trying to figure out what to call Connor.

"So no kayaks?" Lynette asked, remembering what he'd told her.

"Nope. I'm trying to make you love camping, so I figured I'd stack the deck in my favor." Connor chuckled.

Lynette was relieved. She hadn't been ready to kayak again, and she felt as though she'd been given a golden pass to miss the event. "Mister, I think the deck is already stacked in your favor, but please, go right ahead and keep stacking," she teased.

They spent the next hour and a half setting up the tent. The kids were a big help knowing there was a pontoon boat ride at the end of the job. Bingo seemed content to sniff out the wooded areas nearby based on how far his lead would let him go.

By the time she'd dropped Connor off at the marina and drove the truck back to the campsite, it was refreshing to simply sit by the shore and admire the view. An eagle soared overhead, as well as several osprey and hawks. The sounds of the birds calling out in the trees behind her were peaceful, as was the gentle swish of wind that caressed her face.

It was heavenly.

She watched as Connor and the kids pulled close to shore, beaching the boat and tying it off to a tree. He tossed in an anchor at the back to steady the boat and keep it from shifting side to side.

Connor jumped off the bow and came to stand next to her. "Ready to go for a ride?" he asked.

Woof. Woof. Bingo's vote was a resounding yes.

"Absolutely. At least this way, if a snake jumps on the boat, I've got plenty of places to run."

"Right into my arms works for me," Connor said, leaning over to drop a kiss on her cheek.

Lynette blushed. "Works for me too."

"Come on, Bingo. Jump," Gabby called out. The dog didn't have to think about it long before he made the leap.

Connor helped Lynette onto the boat. "I'll be right back. I'm going to grab what we need for hamburgers and some drinks, and then we can head out to cruise the lake and watch the sunset. When we come back, I've got a surprise evening planned for us," he said, jumping back onto shore.

"You're full of surprises, aren't you?"

Connor smiled. "I am, but then a happy man can't help himself."

"So, you are still happy? With everything?" Lynette couldn't help but ask.

"Absolutely. And then some."

"Good. Me too." He squeezed her hand and then turned to walk back up to the site. Bingo jumped off the boat to follow him. It would seem even the dog had fallen in love with Connor.

A beautiful sunset. A beautiful woman. Two kids getting along. A sleepy dog. And a pleasant ride around the lake with the breeze blowing gently. This was Connor's new idea of heaven. The kids swam and played in the bay while he and Lynette cooked up the hamburgers on the beach. He hadn't been kidding when he said this was a much-needed and well-deserved break—for all of them.

The past year had been rough, but as luck would have it, there was a rainbow at the end. A rainbow that came with fair skin, long chestnut hair, and two dimples that made him want to be a better man—and maybe even a husband again.

It had come as a surprise once he understood his feelings for Lynette, and from there they continued to grow deeper. Once upon a time not long ago, he'd sworn he'd never fall in love again or get married. And yet here he was, head over heels for Lynette and considering marriage.

She'd turned his world upside down and then right side up, better than it was before. Connor owed her big time for all that she had done for him and Trey, helping Connor to see and understand what mattered. It was a lesson he'd learned well and one that went far beyond his relationship with his son. And it included Lynette, Gabby, and of course, Bingo. The silly dog chased after everything that moved but always managed to come back when Connor called him.

After the sunset, dusk began to set in and Connor headed back for the campsite. Once they arrived, he cut the engine and floated toward shore. "Hey, Gabby, can you tie us off at the front, and Trey, if you'll toss in the anchor and tighten the line, we should be good." He flipped on the flashlight to help them see what they were doing.

"Yes, sir," Trey said, moving to the stern of the boat to do as instructed.

"Got it, Coach." Not to be outdone, Gabby moved to the bow, more than ready to pitch in and help. "Perfect." Connor took Lynette's hand and helped her ashore.

"Why, thank you, kind sir," she said, grinning.

"My pleasure." He drew her close and dropped a kiss on her cheek, unable to resist. Bingo nudged her hand, wanting attention also.

The kids joined them on shore, each carrying a bag of the stuff that needed to be put away. "Can I start a fire?" Trey asked.

"Not yet. Tonight, I have special plans that involve all of us. Sort of." He chuckled. It paid to do his research on the activity schedule and ask a few questions of the ranger when he'd gone to buy wood.

"I can't wait to hear your idea of fun and special, considering it involves all of us," Trey said, teasing his father.

"Hey, I think I did rather good with the pontoon boat. But tonight, there's a firefly program. You know, the bugs you like to catch and put in a jar to watch them light up?" Connor added as he started to unload the leftover food back to the big cooler.

"You mean the ones you make me release? Of course, I know about fireflies," Trey said, his smile slipping.

Gabby looked from Trey to him and then at her mother. "I've never caught one," she admitted. "Can we?"

"Maybe later. Right now, the ranger is going to do a program to teach you all about them. What it means when they light up and about their life cycle. We see them every summer, but haven't you ever wondered about why they light up?"

"Is it so they can see where they're going?" Lynette asked, teasing Connor.

"Haha. So, I'm sure you know since you're the principal and should know everything. But I thought the kids would like to hear it from an expert."

"Sounds cool by me, but do we have to sit with you? Usually, these programs have a kids group to join in. You know, to give the kids a break from their parents." Trey laughed.

Connor shook his head. "Right, wise guy. More like give the parents a break from the kids," he teased.

"Either way it sounds like fun to me," Gabby chimed in.

"We need to get going as it starts at eight," Connor said. The stars were out in force tonight, and the weather perfect. He grabbed a couple of blankets and flashlights, and then they set out, walking down the road. Several other campers were all headed in the same direction. It would seem tonight's program interested lots of folks.

As they neared the amphitheater, Gabby grabbed Trey's arm. "Look, over there." She pointed at a large group of kids all gathered off to the front right.

"Cool. We'll meet you here after the show," Trey said, the two of them eager to join the other kids.

"That was a smooth move. We have the evening to ourselves. I like it," Lynette said, moving closer and taking his hand. Bingo started forward as if he were going to follow the kids, but instead, he held back, choosing to stick with Lynette.

"I planned it that way. Just you, me, and the stars." A starry night hadn't been anything he could control, but it worked out as though it were a blessing.

"And hundreds of fireflies and lots of people," she teased. Her sense of humor was one of the things that drew him to her. She had a zest for fun and her ability to keep others feeling the same love of life was contagious.

"It'll be our own little world." Connor led her toward the back of the group, where the darkness would give them more privacy. It had the added benefit of being able to see the magical fireflies better. He already knew from having looked up more information on the bugs, that the males and females flashed their lights in a rhythm like a mating ritual. For him, tonight was about a fairy tale setting with a beautiful woman.

He laid out the blanket, Bingo repeatedly trying to lay on it before it was spread out, making the task more difficult. Several other groups of people had the same idea and were setting up not far away—each in their own private world, and yet, together as a group of campers. The ranger, who'd been up near the front and talking to people, took to the stage.

They sat down, side by side, Bingo sprawled out next to Lynette.

"Good evening, folks. Welcome to the Firefly Magic program. I hope you enjoy learning about these fascinating bugs, and, of course, feel free to ask questions by raising your hand. So lie back, keep your eyes on the trees, and listen to the words. We're going to dim the lights so you can see Mother Nature's show better."

"I like the sound of that," Connor said, leaning in close, his voice low. He took her hand and lay back but found it more interesting to watch Lynette than the fireflies.

The ranger went on to tell them in detail the life cycle of the firefly, describing the meaning of the light frequencies of flashes. Over the course of fifteen minutes, they'd become experts on the subject.

"Look at all of them. There must be hundreds. They're so beautiful," Lynette whispered.

Connor's heart surged with love. "As are you."

She turned to face him, her smile radiant in the dim glow of light.

Connor pulled her hand to his lips and pressed a kiss against her skin. "I was hoping tonight worked out as planned because I've got something to tell you. Something important, and I didn't want the kids around to hear it." Bingo lifted his head as if to hear what was being said.

"Connor...please don't tell me you're leaving again?" Lynette asked, her smile disappearing.

He shook his head. "No. Nothing like that. Better. I wanted you alone so that I could tell you this—I love you." Saying the words out loud solidified it in his heart and in his brain. Lynette's sweet answering smile was all the magic Connor needed.

"Well, since you're flashing your light like the fireflies, I reckon I better answer before anyone else here does." She leaned in closer and kissed him. "I love you, too," she murmured.

"*Hmmm*. I like the sound of that," he said, moving to put an arm around her and pulling her close to his side. Bingo edged nearer and planted a doggy lick on Lynette's face, joining in the special moment. Lynette's sweet laughter was like beautiful music. They lay back, perfectly content in that moment. The magic of the evening all around them was breathtaking, just like the woman beside him.

The woman he loved.

Epilogue

One Year Later...

Lynette watched her husband as he corralled the Legal Eagles for a pep talk. Last year, they'd lost the state finals, coming in second place. Pretty darn good for a small-town team from Hallbrook. This year, they were determined not to let the title slip through their fingers.

Bingo sat next to her in the dugout, her days of running around making sure everything was in place, hauling water, and helping with warmups over. Lynette rubbed her belly as the dog nudged her leg.

"The baby is fine, Bingo." It was as though he had a sixth sense her time was drawing close. Soon, baby Miranda would enter the world, and her brother and sister would be amongst the first to greet her.

They were as excited as Connor and helped whenever possible.

Connor's proposal a month after the camping trip hadn't been a surprise. Between the kids and him, she'd known a week before it happened. Giddy smiles and secrets abounded. It was also no surprise he'd insisted Pastor Richard marry them in the church a month later. She loved his enthusiasm to start their life together, something he showed her every day.

The pregnancy, however, *had* come as a surprise. With two very independent older kids in the house, it required an adjustment in their way of thinking, but they were all excited about the new arrival. Connor had converted his study into a little room close to theirs, adding an adjoining door for the baby room. It would be perfect for the first few years, putting off the decision of what to do about more space until further down the road.

Lynette crossed the dugout and stood next to the chain-link fence, trying to get a better view. She rubbed her back, trying to ease the ache. Lately, it felt as though baby Miranda was kicking and punching like she knew she came from a family of athletes.

Connor was just outside the dugout, keeping a close watch on her and the team. Keith covered the third base coaching position. Together, the guys had it all worked out. Her brother was just as protective as her husband. He'd make someone a great husband one day.

"Are you okay, Mrs. Weston?" Teddy asked, coming to stand beside her.

"I'm fine. Why?" she asked, looking down at the young boy. No longer the youngest kid on the team, he'd come out of his shell.

"You just seem agitated. You're either rocking or walking," he teased. "Should I say something to Coach? I mean, you're as big as a house. I remember when my mom had my little sister—she was acting just like you."

Lynette laughed. "I'm fine. Unfortunately, I've got almost two more weeks." She moved to sit on the bench, needing to get off her feet.

"If you say so," Teddy said, shaking his head.

The kid didn't believe her, but the doctor was monitoring her progress. Besides, there were still a few things that needed to be done to finish the baby room—post-season ball games having put a good kink in their schedule.

"Teddy, take over rightfield for Bill," Connor hollered. "This batter likes to hit short and right, so be ready."

Teddy beamed. The kid was excited to be put in a clutch game, having earned the right this past year to be on the field as a frequent secondary. "Thanks, Coach." He stopped by Connor and said something she couldn't hear.

Connor turned and looked back at her, a question in his expression. "You okay, sweetheart?"

"I'm fine. Teddy's a worrywart." Connor's comment explained their conversation. Lynette added a smile, trying to get her husband to return his focus to the game.

By the fourth inning, Lynette wasn't as confident she was fine. The intensity of the contractions had increased. Braxton Hicks wouldn't be this regular and wouldn't keep going this long. She toyed with telling Connor, but the team was only ahead by one run. It was too close of a game to distract him.

Minutes later, a pool of water lay at her feet as her water broke. "*Umm*, Mrs. Weston, I think you better get to the hospital," Andrew said. "My mom's friend had her water break at our house, and unless you peed on yourself, I'm guessing the baby's coming."

Woof. Woof. Woof. Even Bingo understood something was happening. There was no putting off the inevitable anymore. "You're right." She took a few steps closer to her husband. "Connor...I'm sorry, but I think I need to go to the hospital now."

He turned back to her, his surprised expression priceless. "Seriously? I mean...is the baby coming?" he asked, rushing to her side.

"Yes, silly. That is why we need to go. Unless you want to stay and coach. The timing is terrible. Labor can go on for hours. You could stay and finish here and then join me." It wasn't ideal, but these kids deserved their best chance, and Connor was it. Not that Keith was a slacker, but the team idolized their coach.

"No way. Give me a couple of minutes, and we'll leave." He turned back to the field, threw his arm in the air, and called for a time out. Connor headed for home plate to speak with the ump and then waved the team in. The kids gathered around him, and seconds later, they all looked in her direction. They waved at her and smiled, Gabby and Trey running to her side.

"It's really time?" Gabby asked.

"It is," Lynette said, grinning.

"*Ummm*, would it be awful if Gabby and I stayed till the end of the game? For the team, you know," Trey asked. She was proud of Trey for considering all his options and choosing the right one as far she was concerned.

"I insist on it. The baby could take hours, and the team needs you. I think your coach should stay too, but he's having none of it." Lynette hated to do anything that would hurt the Legal Eagle's chances at the win.

Gabby shook her head. "No, he needs to be with you. After all, this is *his* baby too." She grinned, giving Lynette a hug.

"Don't worry, Keith can manage everything, and the team is all in. The other guys want my dad to go to the medical center with you," Trey said, taking control of the situation.

Lynette nodded and let out of sigh of relief. She really did want Connor with her. "Okay, then. I guess it's decided."

"Good luck, Mom," Gabby said. "We'll be there right after the game. I promise. And don't worry about Bingo. We'll make sure he gets home." She patted the dog's head and gave him a kiss.

Lynette kissed her daughter's cheek, trying her best not to show the agony of the next contraction. "Good luck both of you and to the team." She turned to Trey. "You're the captain. In Connor's absence, do your best to lead and to encourage, just like you did last year. Win or lose, you're all amazing. Remember that." It would seem some of Keith's motivational aptitude was rubbing off on her.

"Thanks," Trey said, nodding. "Let's get back out there. We've got a game to win for Coach." His determination would stand him in good stead through life. This past year, they'd all grown close as a family, and it showed in both kids' confidence levels.

Connor jogged over. "Ready?" he asked, reaching for her hand.

"More than," she said, grimacing as another contraction took hold.

Six hours later, baby Miranda made her way into the world. Her tiny toes and feet, and silky soft skin, left Connor weak in the knees. He was proud of his wife, the blessing of his daughter completing their family in a way he hadn't been able to fathom before her arrival.

Holding his little bundle of joy, his heart felt like it would burst. Today was the best day ever. Well, with Lynette around, to be fair, there were a lot of best days ever. But today, not only had Miranda come into the world, but the Legal Eagles had won the state finals.

He stepped into the windowed area that joined the waiting area, surprised to discover the entire team hanging out. Gabby spotted him first, and they all crowded around the glass as he held up baby Miranda.

The team cheered, playfully joking around and jostling each other. As for Connor, he could only smile. He handed the baby to the nurse, waved at the team, and headed back for Lynette's room.

"How's mommy doing?" he asked, his voice soft and filled with love.

"I'm good. Is the baby okay?" she asked.

Connor nodded. "She's perfect. Just like you. I love you, Lynette Weston."

"I love you, too." Lynette's eyes misted with tears, something she did a lot lately. But tears of joy were a-okay with him.

If you enjoyed this sweet and charming romance series, be sure to check out the **ALSO BY ELSIE DAVIS** section on the next page for more clean and wholesome romance.

BONUS READ

Want to keep in touch with new releases and what's happening in the world of Elsie Davis?

Sign up for the monthly newsletter at Elsie Davis HEA (Happily-Ever-After) and enjoy DIGGING THE DRIVER (A Celebrity Corgi Romance) as a FREE BOOK!

The greatest compliment you could give an author is to leave a review in order to help other readers discover the same great stories you enjoyed. Amazon/Bookbub/Goodreads are all great places. Many thanks!!!

Another great way to keep in touch - *Follow Elsie Davis on FaceBook*

Also By Elsie Davis

Sweet, Clean and Wholesome Stories...with a Happily-Ever-After Guarantee!

Holidays in Hallbrook
(Sweet Romance Series for Holidays Throughout the Year)
Welcome to Hallbrook, New Hampshire. A small-town filled with the unexpected, lots of love, and of course, a beloved dog to ramp up the excitement.
Love & Order (Labor Day)
Love & Family (Thanksgiving)
Love & Peace (Christmas)
Love & Chocolate (Valentine's Day)
Love & Hope (Mother's Day)
Love & Liberty (Independence Day)
Love & Honor (Veteran's Day)

Love & Joy (Easter)
Love & Adventure (Father's Day)

Great Smoky Mountain Getaways
(Christian Inspirational – Women's Fiction Ro-
mances)
Juliet's Journey to Love
Poppy's Path to Love
Rachel's Road to Love

Crossroads Creek Cowboys
(Christian Inspirational Romances)
The Heart of a Cowboy
The Help of a Cowboy
The Return of a Cowboy
Coming Soon – The Care of a Cowboy

Crestfield Inn Romances
If you like special kinds of soulmates, a splash of
the supernatural, and wholesome relationships,

you'll adore this sweet bit of fun filled with romance and mystery.
Turning Back Time
Turning Up Roses
Turning Down Pie

Celebrity Corgi Romance
(Standalone Sweet Romance)
If you like light mystery mixed in with your happily-ever-after, you'll enjoy this second-chance romance and the race to save an adorable Corgi.
Digging the Driver

Gold Coast Retrievers
(Sweet Romance)
Special Golden Retrievers help their humans solve mysteries, save lives, and even find love...
Defending Dakota

Trinity River
(Sweet Western Romance)

Ranchers and farmers depend on the Trinity River for water, but when a secret conglomerate starts buying up property by fair means or foul, it's time for the landowners of Tumble County to fight back—Texas style. But what they don't count on, is finding love in the process.
Back in the Rancher's Arms
Small Town, Big Secrets

Coming Soon! (2023-2024)

Sundancer's Legacy – 9 Book series

Sundancer's Star
Sundancer's Joy
Sundancer's Heart
Sundancer's Majesty
Sundancer's Miracle
Sundancer's Glory
Sundancer's Kiss
Sundancer's Moon
Sundancer's Splendor

About The Author

Elsie Davis is a *USA Today and International Bestselling Author* of over 25 sweet, clean, and wholesome romances, and a member of the ACFW. She discovered the world of Happily-Ever-After romance at the age of twelve when she began avidly reading Barbara Cartland, the Queen of Romance, and has been hooked ever since. After building her dream log home on top of a small mountain, she turned her attention to do what she loves most, writing. Elsie writes sweet Contemporary Romance and Contemporary Christian Romance from her heart...hoping to share a little love in a big world.

When she's not writing, she can be found birding, kayaking, camping, fishing, playing disc golf, and taking nature walks—hoping to spot wildlife. Basically, she loves all things outdoors, EXCEPT cold weather. She and her husband are avid Caribbean cruisers, but Elsie's favorite vacation was their cruise to Alaska. (In spite of the cold!) Indoors, she enjoys a toasty fire, and of course, a great romance with a guaranteed Happily-Ever-After.

https://www.elsiedavishea.com

www.ingramcontent.com/pod-product-compliance
Lightning Source LLC
Chambersburg PA
CBHW031627200726
48288CB00019B/305